"You planted flowers for me?" Brady's voice came out rough and uncertain.

"You wouldn't take my money. You painted my house, protected us and took us off the street. Did you think I would just let that pass?" Susanna demanded.

"I didn't ask for payment."

"I know. I wanted to give you something wonderful."

"Something wonderful," he repeated, and his voice was practically a caress. Suddenly the dark seemed warmer, the night turned golden.

"Something magical," she agreed.

"Flowers," he said with disbelief. "What kind of woman comes out at midnight to plant flowers for me?"

"A grateful one," she whispered. "Enjoy the flowers, Brady. They're going to add something nice to your life."

The silence stretched out for several seconds. "You won't come around this late anymore, will you? I'm only a man."

"I won't do it again," Susanna promised. But as for the part about Brady being only a man, he was so very wrong. She was terribly afraid that he was becoming the man she wanted too much.

Dear Reader,

Are you headed to the beach this summer? Don't forget to take along your sunblock—and this month's four new heartwarming love stories from Silhouette Romance!

Make Myrna Mackenzie's *The Black Knight's Bride* (SR #1722) the first book in your tote bag. This is the third story in THE BRIDES OF RED ROSE, a miniseries in which classic legends are retold in the voices of today's heroes and heroines. For a single mom fleeing her ex-husband, Red Rose seems like the perfect town—no men! But then she meets a brooding ex-soldier with a heart of gold....

In *Because of Baby* (SR #1723), a pixie becomes so enamored with a single dad and his adorable tot that she just might be willing to sacrifice her days of fun and frivolity for a human life of purpose...and love! Visit a world of magic and enchantment in the latest SOULMATES by Donna Clayton.

Even with the help of family and friends, this widower with a twelve-year-old daughter finds it difficult to think about the future—until a woman from his past moves in down the street. Rest and relaxation wouldn't be complete without the laughter and love in *The Daddy's Promise* (SR #1724) by Shirley Jump.

And while away the last of your long summer day with *Make Me a Match* (SR #1725) by Alice Sharpe. A feisty florist, once burned by love, is supposed to be finding a match for her mother and grandmother...not falling for the town's temporary vet! Matchmaking has never been so much fun.

What could be better than greeting summer with beach reading? Enjoy!

Mavis C. Allen
Associate Senior Editor

Please address questions and book requests to:
Silhouette Reader Service
U.S.: 3010 Walden Ave., P.O. Box 1325, Buffalo, NY 14269
Canadian: P.O. Box 609, Fort Erie, Ont. L2A 5X3

The Black Knight's Bride

MYRNA MACKENZIE

The Brides of Red Rose

SILHOUETTE *Romance*®

Published by Silhouette Books

America's Publisher of Contemporary Romance

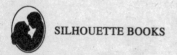

SILHOUETTE BOOKS

ISBN 0-373-19722-5

THE BLACK KNIGHT'S BRIDE

Copyright © 2004 by Myrna Topol

This edition published by arrangement with Harlequin Books S.A.

® and TM are trademarks of Harlequin Books S.A., used under license. Trademarks indicated with ® are registered in the United States Patent and Trademark Office, the Canadian Trade Marks Office and in other countries.

Visit Silhouette Books at www.eHarlequin.com

Printed in U.S.A.

Books by Myrna Mackenzie

MYRNA MACKENZIE,

winner of the Holt Medallion honoring outstanding literary talent, believes that there are many unsung heroes and heroines living among us, and she loves to write about such people. She tries to inject her characters with humor, loyalty and honor, and after many years of writing she is still thrilled to be able to say that she makes her living by daydreaming. Myrna lives with her husband and two sons in the suburbs of Chicago. During the summer she likes to take long walks, and during cold Chicago winters, she likes to *think* about taking long walks (or dream of summers in Maine). Readers may write to Myrna at P.O. Box 225, LaGrange, IL 60525, or they may visit her online at www.myrnamackenzie.com.

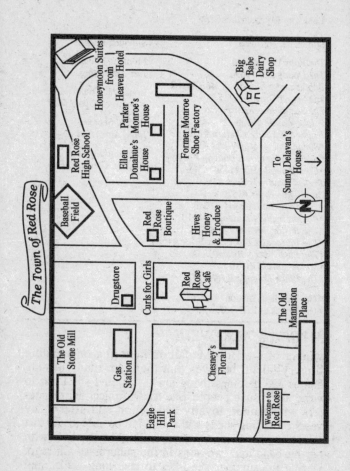

The Town of Red Rose

The Old Stone Mill
Gas Station
Eagle Hill Park
Chesney's Floral
Welcome to Red Rose
The Old Manniston Place
Drugstore
Curls for Girls
Red Rose Café
Red Rose Boutique
Hives Honey & Produce
Baseball Field
Red Rose High School
Honeymoon Suites from Parker Heaven Hotel
Ellen Donahue's House
Monroe's House
Former Monroe Shoe Factory
To Sunny Delavan's House →
Big Babe Dairy Shop
N

Chapter One

"We're okay, sweetie. Don't worry. We're all right." Susanna Wright tried to steer the limping car into the soft gravel at the side of the road and almost managed to do that before the car gave its last wheeze. She heard the hint of desperation in her voice as she whispered the words to her twelve-month-old daughter, Grace, sleeping soundly in the back seat. She wanted to wish for a miracle but suppressed the desire. Miracles didn't tend to come her way. At least, they hadn't for a long time.

"We're fine," she said again. Maybe Grace didn't need the reassurance but Susanna did. The sky had already gone dark, they hadn't reached their destination, and she didn't know what was wrong with the car. Worse than that, there didn't seem to be much of anything out here except for a glow from one small house sitting about thirty feet off the road. Who knew what she'd find if she banged on the door of that house? And what if she didn't like what she found there? With a broken car, a baby and two miles of seemingly unlit road between her and her destination, the town of Red Rose, Illinois, just where would she run to? Better to just lie low here in the car and wait until morning.

She had just turned from taking her sleeping daughter from the car seat and settled her into her arms when something hit the roof of her car with a thump.

Susanna shrieked and pulled her baby tighter.

Grace started to cry.

The something that had landed on her car scratched away at the cloth top and leaped off the car, hustling into the dark in the direction of the lighted house.

Almost immediately a barking and snarling began. The sound of metal clattering added to the noise, and the barking grew more frantic, deep-throated and threatening.

Suddenly light flooded the yard in front of the house. A tall man stepped outside.

"Stay, Scrap. Be still," he said in a voice as low and calm as any Susanna had ever heard. "Let's see what you have there." He bent on one knee and shone a light under the porch. "Just a raccoon, Scrap, probably trying to get into the garbage can. Drive you nuts, don't they? Come on into the house for a few minutes. It's not going to leave until you do, and you're not going to be quiet until it's gone."

The dog kept barking, the sound harsh and belligerent.

"Scrap," the man commanded in a lower, sterner voice.

The dog whimpered once, then subsided.

In the silence Grace let out a lusty cry.

Scrap barked again.

The flashlight swung in an arc, illuminating the car, trapping Susanna in its beam. Her breath lodged in her chest somewhere, hurting her, but she couldn't let it out.

She couldn't see the man for the glare of the light now shining in her face, either, but she could hear his quiet command to his dog to stay and she could hear his footsteps crunching on the ground as he moved nearer. The light of the flashlight bounced a bit, but remained on her face as she finally dragged air into her lungs in a shaky breath. The windows were closed, the car doors were locked, but she remembered her first glimpse of the man when he'd emerged from the house. He was tall with linebacker shoulders. A flimsy car window wouldn't be a match for him.

Slowly she started to edge over to the passenger seat, but she bumped up against Grace's car carrier that she had moved there after they had stopped. It effectively blocked her way.

The footsteps came closer.

"Ma'am?" the man asked.

She didn't answer.

"Are you all right in there?" he added.

She considered maintaining her silence, but to what purpose? If she didn't say anything, he would, no doubt, keep moving closer.

"I—we're fine." She managed to get the words out. "We just stopped to rest. We'll be going in a minute. Now, actually." With Grace still on her lap, Susanna turned the key, praying that the few minutes of downtime had been enough to fix whatever had been wrong. She didn't like leaving Grace unbelted, but at the moment the man seemed the larger threat to her child's safety. She would fasten her baby in properly once they were out of his sight.

But though she tried several times, the engine would not turn over and Susanna realized her mistake then. Both she and the man knew she had no way out of here.

"I don't think that car is going anywhere, ma'am," the man said quietly, but she noticed that he backed away a step. The slight gesture helped her breathe just a bit easier.

She pulled the key out of the ignition and struggled for composure. "Could you— Would you be able to call a tow truck in town?"

"Not a problem." He pulled a portable phone from his pocket and started to move forward.

"No," she said too suddenly, not wanting him to get that close. "You—you're from around here. You probably know the right place to call. Could you do it?"

There was a pause. She wished she was the one holding the light so she could see his expression, but he finally moved and punched in a number. He hit a button and she could hear the ringing, but there was no answer.

He dialed another number. "Ms. Woolverton, there's a stranded lady that needs a tow out at Malone Woods," he said. Susanna noted that he didn't identify himself in any way, and his voice was devoid of expression. He listened for what seemed like a long time. "Then when someone is available," he said, and severed the connection.

"It might be some time," he told Susanna.

She took a deep breath. "We'll be fine. I— Could I ask you— There's a hotel in town, the Red Rose

Heaven, but I couldn't get a room when I called up earlier. Is there another place I could try?''

"No. No other place, and you're right about not being able to get a room at the Red Rose now. The town is crawling with strangers this weekend. A festival or something. Full.''

She nodded. She hadn't really wanted to stay at the hotel, anyway. The prices were higher than she could safely afford. None of this was working out the way she had dreamed when she had first read the reprinted story from the *Red Rose Gazette* on the Internet. A town with lots of women and very few men, a place where she would just be another female among many, a place so different from her own big-city background that no one would think to look for her here.

Initially, her thoughts had just been musings, far-fetched daydreams in which she arrived in Red Rose in broad daylight, found some way to set herself up and got a job. Any job. She hadn't meant to actually do any of those things, but then Trent, her ex-husband, had shown up at her door. As if they hadn't been divorced for a year. He'd been doing that a lot lately, and each time had been ugly, frightening, even though he'd never physically threatened her. This time was worse. He had intimated that he had changed his mind about never wanting Grace. He had spun several scenarios where he could coerce Susanna into taking him back, making her feel cornered, knowing there was nothing she could really do to keep him away. At least, nothing truly effective. He had the money and the influence to do lots of things. Trent knew people, and some of them might actually help him. He might try to take Grace for real, if only for spite or to force Susanna to come back to him.

And suddenly scared in a way she hadn't been before, Susanna was throwing things in her car and heading down the road with no destination in mind until her thoughts had cleared out just a bit and she'd pointed the car in this direction. Now, here she was, in a dark, deserted place far outside the town, facing a strange man more than a head taller than Trent.

"Ma'am, your baby's crying."

Susanna took a deep breath to keep from crying, too. "I just have to feed her." She relaxed somewhat when she realized that he wasn't moving any closer to the car.

"Can I give you a lift into town, miss?" He said the words gently but without enthusiasm, as if he was as exasperated by the situation as she was.

And get into the car with a strange man? Possibly put Grace in greater danger?

"We'll be fine," she said, realizing that the phrase was fast becoming her mantra. "If we could just stay here in the car until the tow truck comes...."

The light bounced as if he had nodded. He didn't bother inviting her into his house, and she wondered if he didn't want her there or if he simply realized she wouldn't accept. "That's fine," he said in that deep, gritty voice. He started to turn back toward his house. "Come, Scrap," he said, and his tone held a note of affection. She supposed it had been there all along, but her fear had prevented her from noting it before.

"Thank you, Mr...." She hesitated. He didn't fill in the blank. "I'm sorry, but I don't know your name," she said.

He stopped in his tracks, but he didn't turn around.

"Malone," he said, his voice clipped, and then he started walking again.

"Thank you, Mr. Malone."

She watched him as he returned to his house. He walked with a slight limp, but an economy of movement otherwise, very straight and tall. She stared after him as he started to move inside the door. He paused, looking in her direction for the briefest of minutes, caught in the light from the house. She realized that he had short, dark hair. His jaw was clean-shaven, his nose like a blade. Everything about him was lean and hard. Except for the expression in his eyes, which was...unreadable. For just a second there, staring at this man who was the epitome of masculinity, something inherently feminine awakened and shivered through her. An unwelcome something. She had had enough of male dominance in her life. What she wanted was a rest, a reprieve before she moved on and made a place for herself and Grace far away from her roots and her past. She didn't want to recognize whatever elemental something in this man that evoked a purely female and involuntary reaction.

And she didn't have to. In just a minute he and Scrap had disappeared inside the house. He left the light burning, and she wondered if it was for her sake or if he'd simply forgotten to turn it off. Probably forgotten. The light didn't quite reach the car, anyway.

Quickly she fed her baby, cuddled her close for a few minutes, then put her back into her car seat to sleep. The dark and the stress of the day overtook her and Susanna felt the world slip away.

She awoke with a start. Sitting in the cramped car seat, she had fallen half over, and her body jerked her out of sleep. She blinked several times as reality set in and she remembered where she was.

There was still no sign of the tow truck.

But sitting on the hood of the car was a battery-powered lantern, a pillow, two blankets and a box.

Glancing around warily, Susanna realized that it really was just her and Grace and the night out here.

She slid open the door and hauled the things inside. Flipping open the box, she found a sandwich and a thermos of milk.

"Thank you, Mr. Malone," she whispered after she had eaten the sandwich and had done her best to make herself comfortable with the blanket and pillow. She tucked the other blanket half over Grace's car seat.

She wondered if her Mr. Malone would come outside when the tow truck arrived so that she could thank him properly and return the things she'd borrowed.

But when she awoke the next time to the sound of an engine beside her car, it was already morning, and the man in the house was nowhere in sight.

After he'd seen the woman take the food and provisions into her car, Brady Malone kept a vigil by the door, watching for the tow truck driver. Not that he thought Nate Fisher was going to show up anytime soon. Nate had a grudge against Brady going back eleven years when they'd both been fifteen and Brady had busted his nose for the second time. It was one of many grudges various members of the town had against Brady, most of them well-deserved. But Brady hadn't had the heart to tell the woman that she was going to have a long wait. No doubt Nate would give her the details of his history with Brady when and if he showed up. And if she spent more than a few hours in Red Rose, she would, no doubt, be given a few details about the history of the Malones.

Absentmindedly, Brady stretched out his long legs and rubbed his right knee. There would be rain soon. The three-year-old wound was as good a barometer as any made by man. At least something slightly useful had come out of the stateside accident that had taken the life of a good man and ended Brady's military career. He hoped the rain stayed away until the woman was gone. Looked as though she had enough trouble without mud making her ordeal in the car even more unpleasant.

"If I fall asleep and someone comes, wake me, Scrap," he told his dog. Hearing his name, Scrap lifted his big black head, a patient look in his eyes. He probably knew as well as Brady did that neither one of them would fall asleep again tonight. Not when there were innocents to watch over.

The woman and the baby now? That might be a different story. He hoped she'd sleep. She had been beyond scared, with big green eyes framed by a mass of tousled blond hair, neither of which did a thing to make her look tough, although she'd done her best to overcome her vulnerable appearance and to mask her fear. He admired her attempt at bravery in a situation where any woman alone would feel herself at risk. She looked to be a couple of years younger than himself, Brady guessed. Which meant she couldn't be more than twenty-three or twenty-four.

"Can't blame her for being scared, Scrap," he said. "Alone with a baby on a deserted road and a man peering into her car. I wonder what she's doing here."

Not that he was going to find out. Eventually, after

Nate had made his point that Brady didn't order him around, he would show up to tow her car. And then the woman would disappear into the town proper.

And since Brady stayed out of Red Rose and away from its inhabitants except when absolutely necessary, he would probably never see that pretty blond lady or her baby again.

Which was just as well, all things considered.

Susanna didn't bother to ask the sour-faced tow truck driver what had taken him so long to get here. It was obvious by the look on his face that he wasn't happy to be here even now.

He looked at the black convertible she was driving and the Chicago city sticker on the windshield. "Ninety dollars gets you to town," he said.

The town was only a couple of miles away.

But her car was completely inoperable. She mentally measured the contents of her wallet and gave a tight nod.

The man began to hook the chains to her car. "I hear Brady Malone called this in," he said. There was no friendliness to his voice.

"Yes," she said and sudden anger flooded her. She didn't know why this man was so unfriendly or what was between him and the man in the house, but she knew one thing. Brady Malone had not made her feel as if she was a bother. He had made sure she and Grace had had blankets and food.

The man was almost done with the chains.

"Excuse me, I'll just be a minute," Susanna suddenly said. Propping Grace on her hip, she draped the blankets over her free arm and picked up the box containing the empty thermos and set off toward the house.

"Gotta be back in town in fifteen minutes," the tow truck driver yelled. "Ain't got time to wait."

Susanna didn't turn around. "You'll be there," she said, and kept walking. Coming up to the house, she pounded on the door. A few seconds later it opened enough to reveal Brady Malone.

She looked up and realized that he was even taller than she'd thought, a full head taller than she was. In the burgeoning daylight, she could see that his eyes were dark blue. He was frowning.

"I wouldn't take chances with Nate," he said. "He'd just as soon leave you here as wait for you."

She bit her lip. "I just wanted to give you these," she said, holding out the box and blankets. "And to thank you."

He gave a curt nod. "You're welcome, ma'am."

"Susanna Wright," she said.

"All right, then, you're welcome, Susanna Wright," he agreed.

"It was nice meeting you, too, Brady Malone," she said, supplying the nicety that he had omitted.

Something that was almost a smile flitted across his lips. "I see Nate filled you in on my first name. I won't ask what else he told you."

"Nothing." But she heard the tow truck's engine rev behind her.

"Better go."

"I'll see you."

He raised one brow. "You're staying in Red Rose?"

"I hope so. Wish me luck in finding a job."

But he only gestured toward the tow truck and

didn't answer. She wondered what that meant. And it occurred to Susanna as she rode into town, seated next to the frowning Nate, that she had come to Red Rose because she'd read that there weren't many men here, and yet the only people she'd met so far had been male. One who was grumpy, she thought, glancing at the man driving the truck, and one who was...intriguing. Brady Malone hadn't seemed very pleased that she was thinking of staying in his town.

What was this Red Rose like, anyway?

Chapter Two

The Internet was a fine thing, Brady thought later that day. He had received computer training in the army and that had enabled him to make a living designing computer software for businesses when he had returned home after the accident that had resulted in his injury. He conducted most of his business from home, dealing with small firms in St. Louis and other parts of the country, never Red Rose, and he managed to make a decent living that way.

But it was the Internet and the town's message board that enabled him to keep his finger on the pulse of the area without ever having to venture into town. If he cared to take a look, that was. Most of the time he didn't. The message board tended to be gossipy, and he had always considered gossip to be fodder for his enemies. He stayed away for the most part and only concentrated on the informational portions of the town's Web site. Today, however, curiosity about his midnight visitors found him scanning the message board. Susanna Wright was a stranger to Red Rose and, in a town this size, anyone new tended to cause a stir.

Which was how he knew within minutes of its happening that she had gotten into some sort of a disagreement with Nate Fisher on the ride into town and Nate had ended up insisting that he had quoted her ten dollars more than she claimed he had. Brady felt the heat of anger rising through him at that. He and Nate were at odds, but at least *he* wasn't an innocent. Susanna Wright had done nothing to merit Nate's scummy ways. He resumed reading.

The posts went on with Evangelina Purcell, who ran the gas station and knew Nate's ways better than most people, and Sunny Delavan, who knew almost everything Evangelina didn't know, speculating on what had happened:

"Then things got worse. Nate refused to turn the lady's car over to her unless she paid up." Evangelina supplied that tidbit. *"I thought my teeth would fall out and I don't even have dentures."*

"The slimy son of a snake," Sunny added. *"So what did she do?"*

"Well, she tried to argue at first, kind of gentle-like, you know," Evangelina wrote. *"But then when a few people stopped to look, she backed off and paid him the extra ten dollars."*

"I wouldn't have paid him," Sunny wrote.

"Yes, well, we all know you're capable of handling any man, Sunny," Evangelina told her. *"This woman is a stranger, and she looked kind of fragile."*

Brady agreed wholeheartedly. Susanna Wright did seem fragile and innocent and gentle. And very frightened. He wished that Nate were here in person, so he could show him just what he thought of a man who attacked a woman, and Nate's methods definitely qualified as an attack. But Sunny was already answering. Brady read on.

"*Then what happened?*" Sunny asked.

"*Nate told her that he ran the only repair shop in town and that she needed a fuel pump. I think he even laughed, although that might have been just my imagination. He always looks like he's either scowling or leering, and I was just too mad to concentrate.*"

"*I'll bet he quoted her some ridiculous price, too.*"

"*He did,*" Evangelina agreed. "*I'm sure it was his 'you're-from-out-of-town' price. That poor young woman's face turned paper-white. She looked as if she might faint.*"

"*Well, can you blame her?*" Sunny wrote. "*Nate's a first-class jerk, and he acts like a double-first-class jerk to those people who live outside this town. He figures you've got no choice but to do business on his terms.*"

"*And it's true,*" Evangelina typed. "*Without a repair that poor woman's car was just another dead rust bucket. What could she do?*"

"*So she went along????*" Sunny asked, the words appearing on Brady's screen, the extra question marks obvious signs of consternation. Brady remembered Sunny as a woman of action. She probably hated not being able to do anything about this situation.

"*Sure, she went along. Then Nate, the lowlife, told her he'd put her car into the lineup, and you know what that means.*"

Sunny keyed in a frowning icon. "*Yeah, I know darn well what it means. It means she's going to have to wait, probably hours, even if Nate, the mean old coot, doesn't have any other cars to fix. Wouldn't you just like to smack him with his own tire iron? That poor young thing is going to have to cool her heels while Nate plays high and mighty, or my name isn't Sunny.''*

At that point, Delia Sable, who worked at the flower shop and had *''just checked in for a second to see what was going on,''* joined the posting.

''That Nate doesn't even deserve to be called a man,'' she wrote. *''We should just kick him out of town, the meanie.''* Which were pretty fierce words for a woman who was known to be a shy and gentle soul.

Brady pondered what he had just read as the women moved on to other topics. He clicked off the site. No doubt Susanna Wright was already sorry that she'd ever even heard of Red Rose.

Which would mean she would be leaving soon, a fact that shouldn't mean a thing to him.

Except Evangelina's description of the woman's white face and sick expression hit him right in the gut. She didn't deserve that kind of treatment. It reminded him that her car, though it had once been expensive, was also getting up there in years. Even by flashlight, he had seen that there were a few dents and a fair amount of rust and that the tires were going bald. She wasn't a woman who could afford to throw money away. And she had that baby to care for.

Brady considered the possibilities. He hated going into town and avoided it whenever possible.

But man, he *really* didn't like Nate Fisher. There was nothing like getting even with an old enemy.

With a long, slow movement, Brady flipped off the

computer and rose to his feet. He called Scrap and
the two of them headed out to the truck.

Susanna sat on one of the two hard-plastic orange
chairs at the repair station and ran her fingers over
the chipped-away edge of the seat. She held Grace
who was kicking her feet and seemingly happy. But
then Grace hadn't had to deal with that awful man.

"Well, at least there's one good thing, sweetie,"
Susanna said. "I had his number from the start." Susanna's poor batting average with men was a sore spot
with her. Starting with her father whom she had un-
successfully tried to please until the day he died, and
continuing on through Trent who had wanted to cut
her off from the rest of the world, she had always had
this terrible habit of thinking the men in her life were
more noble than they really were. That tendency had
left her heartbroken and disillusioned one too many
times. At least with Nate Fisher, she had known he
was a stinker from the first moment she'd met him.

"This isn't exactly what I'd planned, Grace," Susanna whispered to her babbling daughter as she
peered out the window and saw Nate Fisher disap-
pearing into what looked to be a drugstore of some
sort. "I just wanted a safe place to rest and to hide
before we moved on. This seemed a likely haven."

Trent, with the surly attitude he'd developed the
past couple of years, had driven away the few female
friends Susanna had made. Red Rose, with its seem-
ing deficiency of males, had seemed like a good place
to settle and to fix what had gone wrong with her life.
She had wanted to see how other women lived. Instead, she had yet to meet even one female. She
wasn't going to count the ones who had witnessed

her distressing experience when Nate Fisher had charged her extra for the tow and then explained that she was dependent on him to fix her car.

Where on earth was she going to get the money to live once she had paid the bill for this car repair? She had thought she had enough to make a start, to find a job at least, but already this new emergency had cut into her meager savings. Maybe she shouldn't have told the lawyer that she didn't want to argue money during her divorce. She had just wanted to be free of Trent and his bullying ways, and adding money and support payments would have meant having to deal with him for a great many years. It would have given him power over her, and her ex-husband's love of power was what had driven her away. No matter. What was done was done. She was left with very little money.

So this time Susanna couldn't even begin to tell her daughter that they would be fine. Instead she hugged her baby and kissed her soft cheek. She would do whatever she had to do to make a better life for Grace.

Turning her back to the window, Susanna prepared to wait for Nate Fisher. She didn't dare try to figure out what she would say if he tried to charge her even more than he had quoted for the repair.

"I don't know, but it's just not going to happen," she said. "There are limits to even a nice woman's patience."

She heard a footfall on the concrete outside the station and turned quickly, figuring that it was her sadistic repairman. Instead, Brady Malone stood there, staring down at her. His blue eyes were like an electric force. She could swear that he could see secret parts of her that she wanted kept hidden, but she was powerless to stop him from looking.

And she couldn't seem to look away. Her heart did some funny acrobatic move that she didn't want to examine.

"Mr. Malone?" she said in a voice that was weaker than she would have liked.

"I heard you had a fuel pump problem, and that Nate was most likely dealing in a little price gouging."

Susanna blinked. "You— How did you hear that?"

He shrugged but didn't look repentant. "It's a small town. No secrets. At least not many."

She wondered what that meant, if he knew any of her other secrets. But no, he couldn't. No one here knew her at all.

"Yes, well, I'm dealing with it," she said, a trifle defensively.

He almost smiled then. "You managed to get him to go lower on the price, then?"

A flood of warmth swept up her face. "I don't really know exactly what it should cost to fix a fuel pump."

"I do, and even if I didn't, I can guarantee that Nate would try to overcharge you."

A trace of anger racketed through her. "So what do most people do when he quotes them an unfair price?"

"I'm not sure. I would guess that most of them would tell him to go to hell. Or at least that's what I'd tell him if I needed him to fix my car. As it is, I just don't talk to him."

"What do you do when you need your car fixed?"

"If it's something I can't do myself, I take it to the

next closest town, or even St. Louis, if it's still drivable. If the repair is something I know how to fix, that's not an issue.''

Grace let out a cooing sound, smacking her lips and turning big blue trusting eyes up to Brady at that moment. Susanna was almost sure he leaned back, as if the baby could somehow hurt him.

Quickly he turned his attention to Susanna. ''As it happens, I know how to change a fuel pump.'' He stared at her, a speculative look in his eyes.

Susanna didn't hesitate. ''How much?''

He shook his head slowly. ''Just the pure naked joy of making Nate lose his temper.''

She wasn't sure how she felt about that. She didn't like Nate Fisher, but revenge had never been a motivating factor for her, especially since Trent seemed to use revenge as his reason for making her life a misery. Still, what was between Nate Fisher and Brady Malone obviously ran deep. It was Nate's comment on the drive in to town that she had better be careful about hanging around with white trash that had set Susanna off in the first place. Her simple but cool, ''I don't like the term white trash, and Mr. Malone was very kind to me,'' had elicited a sneer and a sullen curse from Nate. She suspected her attitude was the reason he had overcharged her.

''I have to pay you something,'' she argued.

He hesitated. ''We'll discuss it when I'm done and you're satisfied that your car is running.''

She shook her head. ''I appreciate the fact that you're helping me, but I like to have things set out in black and white from the first. It's important that I not have any surprises. I've already had one today.''

''Fair enough. Let's say twenty-five dollars.''

Her eyes widened. "That's hardly fair to you. Fifty, and I pay for the parts." Which was such a stupid thing to say, when money was so scarce. But really, she didn't want to be beholden to any man. Not ever again. It was important to her. And besides, even she knew that fifty dollars was far too low a price for the work this was going to entail. Still, she needed the illusion that she was partially in control for once.

Brady braced his big hands on the door frame and looked to the side. She was pretty sure that he was counting to ten.

"Please," she said, and he blinked.

"Don't do that."

"Do what?"

"Don't beg. I said I'd do it. And even if I don't like your terms, I still will. Where's your car?" he asked. "Behind the shop?"

She nodded. "But it's not running. And if we have to get it towed…"

"We won't. Get in and put it in neutral. I'm going to push it into the street. That's all we need, to get it off of Fisher's property."

"You're going to work on it on a public street? Can you do that?"

She almost thought that the man was going to smile. A small light came into those dark blue eyes. "I don't imagine that it's a hanging offense."

"But you might get a ticket."

"Wouldn't be my first. Won't be my last."

She hesitated.

"Ms. Wright, let's do this thing, all right? I have work waiting for me when I get home."

And like that, she flew to her car, belted Grace into her carrier, and put the car in neutral, doing her best to guide it according to Brady's instructions as he pushed the vehicle out into the street.

"Now what?" she asked when the car was in place.

"Now you go over to the gas station, ask Evangelina, the owner, to call the auto parts place in Lindley Junction and have them send out a new fuel pump for your car. I'll start removing the old one. Then you take your baby and go into the café. I'll bet you haven't eaten yet. Don't worry. We'll have you back on the road in no time."

Susanna blinked. "I wasn't exactly thinking of getting back on the road. Grace and I are going to visit here for a while."

He raised his brows at that. "You know people here?" His voice was incredulous. Of course. If she'd known people, why was she depending on him for help?

"I don't know anyone yet," she confessed, "but I've read about this town. I like to garden and there was a small article reprinted on the Internet about one of your citizens who is a landscaper. A friend forwarded it to me. It mentioned Red Rose's attempts to get men to move here, and made the town seem like a nice place, a place that has plans and is trying to grow and change. That's me, too, a woman trying to grow and change. So, when I hit one of those crossroads in life that come along now and then, I thought I'd come see what it was really like, get a job and stay here awhile."

"Until you reach a new crossroad."

"Exactly." Susanna tried to smile, even though she thought that Brady found her attitude amusing and naive. Heck, even she conceded that her attitude was amusing and naive, but she desperately needed a place to hole up for a short time. Why not here?

Maybe because she still didn't have a job or a place to stay?

"Could you do one more thing for me and point me in the direction of any apartments that might be for rent?" she asked.

Brady sighed. "This isn't exactly an apartment kind of town."

Maybe she really was naive. Maybe she should have stayed around Chicago until she had all her chickens in a row.

But Trent had been slipping into her apartment when she was away from home. He wasn't a physically threatening kind of man, but still…

She eyed her car. What was one more night sleeping in it? Grace was so small, she could sleep anywhere.

Brady took a step nearer. He let out a long, slow breath. "Don't even think of sleeping in there," he said as if he had read her mind. "If you really need a place to stay, I have an outbuilding that will do for a few days. It's furnished. I used to stay there at times when I was a teenager. Nothing fancy, but habitable."

She got the feeling that he didn't really want to offer it to her. And the truth was that she really didn't want to stay that near him. She was trying to decrease her dependence on men, not increase it. That fact and her pride almost made her turn him down, but there was Grace to consider. She didn't really want to make her baby sleep in a car.

Susanna gave a tight nod. "I hesitate to ask, but it's important for me to know…"

"It's not much. I'd give it to you for free, but you'd

probably just argue. Let's make it ten dollars a night," he said flatly, without asking what she had meant. Again, not really a fair price, but she was getting the distinct impression that Brady Malone was sorry he had met her and been forced to play the Good Samaritan.

"Thank you," she said. "We'll only be there as long as it will take for me to get a job and find something more permanent. I promise we won't be any trouble." But then, that was a bit of a rash statement to make. Brady Malone had been sitting home minding his own business last night when she had rolled into his life. And it was obvious that she had already been a lot of trouble.

Thank goodness he was a very generous kind of man.

"Let me get this straight? Brady Malone is repairing your car?" Susanna sat in the Red Rose Café and looked up at a big-boned woman who was staring at her incredulously.

"Ye-es," she said hesitantly. "Is there some problem with that? Is he incapable of making the repair?"

The woman, who had introduced herself as Sunny Delavan, the owner of the Big Babe Dairy Shop, glanced across to Lydia Eunique, the mayor and owner of the café.

Lydia let out a deep breath. "Honey, most of us here have known Brady all his life, and we don't know half of what he's capable of. He probably can fix your car, no problem. The question is, *why* is he doing it? It's just not his way."

Susanna could feel the tension flooding the room. "Why not? He offered."

"Yes, and that's definitely not his way, either," Sunny said. "Brady doesn't offer to do things for people. He doesn't hardly ever even step foot in the town. He definitely doesn't get involved with the women here." She gave Susanna a pointed look.

Susanna hoped she wasn't blushing. "Oh, it's not like that at all," she insisted. "Besides, I'm the last woman who wants to get involved with a man."

It was as if a communal meaningful look passed over the room. Susanna frowned. She was beginning to get angry.

"Don't mind us," a soft-spoken woman said. "Your statement was just a bit of déjà vu for some of us. I'm Abigail Chesney, by the way," she said.

Susanna brightened. "Yes, I read an article about you. It made Red Rose sound like a very nice place."

Abigail smiled. "Yes, well the reporter who wrote it is somewhat partial to the town, as are we all, but the point is that only a few weeks ago I stood here and said the same thing as you just did, that I didn't want to get involved with a man."

"So did I," a gentle-eyed waitress said. "I'm Ellie Donahue. And we didn't mean to be rude, but Abby and I both declared that we didn't want a man, and yet only weeks later, we both find ourselves engaged to be married. My fiancé, Parker Monroe, is responsible for trying to lure businessmen to the town with his open houses. We're having another one this weekend. And Abby's fiancé, Griffin O'Dell, has upgraded one of the stately old properties and is bringing clients here, which can only be good for Red Rose. The point is, that if you're a woman in Red Rose, and you claim that you don't want a man, no one's likely to believe you anymore."

Susanna frowned harder.

"But they're not going to censure you, either," Abby said. "Here in the Red Rose Café, any woman can say anything she likes, and the rest of us will back her up one hundred per cent, no matter what we personally believe. So if you say that there's absolutely nothing going on between you and Brady, we're just going to take that on faith."

Which won a grateful smile from Susanna. "Good, because my ex-husband pretty much soured me on men. I can't risk ever going through that again, especially not when I have Grace to look out for."

"She's a sweet little love," Lydia said as Grace blew raspberries and smiled at her. "You're right to be cautious."

"Yes," Sunny agreed. "Especially where Brady is concerned. You be careful around him, all right? The Malone men have caused a ton of trouble and heartache in this town over the years. They're hard men to read, and even harder to recover from when something bad happens. And generally speaking, something bad always happens when a Malone man is around."

Susanna noticed some frowns from the women gathered here, but no one refuted Sunny's words.

"I intend to be incredibly careful," she said, sipping her coffee. "And I only intend to live on his property until I find another place to stay. Are there any apartments available right now?"

Sunny scratched her head. "Not many apartments here. There are those new ones over in Lindley Junction, but I've heard they're charging an outrageous rent."

"How much is outrageous?" Susanna asked, thinking that what was expensive here might not seem like that much to a former Chicagoan.

Sunny rattled off a price and Susanna almost choked on her coffee. "I'll keep looking," she said. "How about work? Are there any jobs available in town right now?"

"It depends," Ellie said. "What kind of job do you want?"

"Any job."

Lydia raised an eyebrow.

"I mean it," Susanna insisted. "As I pointed out, I have a baby to care for. I'd welcome anything that would put food on the table."

"Well, in that case," Lydia said, "we might have something here." She looked at Ellie.

"As I mentioned, I'm getting married," Ellie said. I was planning on working a few more weeks, mostly because Lydia didn't have anyone to take my place."

"She doesn't really need to work, though," Sunny confided. "Parker's rich as sin."

"So if you don't mind waiting tables, the job is yours right away," Ellie said.

Turning to Lydia, Susanna nodded. "What do you need to know about me?"

Lydia smiled. "Can you pour a cup of coffee?" She waited.

"I think I can handle that," Susanna answered with a smile of her own.

"Good. Then you can start as soon as you're settled in tomorrow. And at the beginning, you can bring the baby with you. I can set up a playpen in the back."

Susanna blinked. "Thank you. I think I love Red Rose already."

Sunny let out a deep, throaty laugh. "We'll see. You haven't spent a night with Brady Malone yet."

"I won't be staying *with* him," Susanna protested. "I'll be living in an outbuilding on his property."

Sunny gave her the look; that "Come-on,-honey,-be-realistic" look. "Lady, I don't know Brady well, but I know he gives off male vibrations that travel well beyond the bounds of his property. He was a military man, and he looks it. Most women can't resist that look or that magnetism, at least if they get within close range. It looks like you're going to be plenty close enough."

"Maybe. I'll give you the fact that he's handsome," Susanna said.

Lydia nodded.

"And he does exude this kind of... I don't know, this sensual draw," Susanna added.

"Definitely," Abby agreed.

"I'll bet he knows what to do with a woman and a bed," one woman added.

"Joyce," Ellie chided gently, but Susanna noticed that she smiled.

"Well, he does look good," Susanna agreed a bit nervously, "But I'm made of pretty stern stuff. To start casting cow eyes at Brady would be the height of foolishness." Not to mention that the very thought scared the stuffing out of her. Brady sounded like a man who liked his isolation. Like Trent, a man she hoped never to see again.

At that moment the door opened, the bell jangling out of control. Brady stood there, tall and dangerous-looking.

Susanna wondered where her breath had gone. Her lungs certainly weren't working properly.

"You can't be done already," she said, somehow finding her voice.

"I'm not. Evangelina just called and told me that they don't have the part in Lindley Junction. I'll have to go farther afield, and it may take a bit longer," he said.

"That's fine. I'll just wait here," she said, wishing she could look away from his eyes.

Brady nodded. He avoided looking at anyone else in the room, and closed the door behind him as he left.

Susanna felt as if her heart was jumping around in her body. She noticed that some of the other women were looking a bit faint themselves.

"What was that you said about not making cow eyes at Brady?" Lydia asked.

"Moo," Sunny replied.

Susanna gave her a don't-get-started look. She might as well begin as she meant to go on. "Why don't I just put on an apron and get to work right now," she offered. "I am, after all, here to work, and that's all," she said firmly, daring anyone to argue with her.

They didn't.

But deep inside, Susanna knew that she wasn't out of danger. Words alone didn't make a woman safe. If the man was compelling enough, there was always danger.

And Brady was definitely compelling. When he'd walked out the door, her whole body had snapped to attention and she'd been tempted to follow him out into the street.

Even now, she couldn't help wondering what it would be like living on his property, when she already knew how dark and deserted his land was. It would be as if the two of them were the only adults in the world, just one man and one woman.

And in only a few hours, she would be living with that feeling. Every night.

Chapter Three

Several hours later Brady was cleaning the grease off of his hands. He looked across the street to the window of the Red Rose Café and saw that Lydia was staring out at him. She probably wondered what in hell he thought he was doing. Well, she wasn't the only one. He wondered the same thing. A smart man would have simply stayed at home today, and while he was many undesirable things, he wasn't dumb. He'd known he was stepping into a puddle of trouble when he had followed Susanna Wright to town.

Damn Nate Fisher for forcing his hand. And damn himself for allowing himself to be forced, Brady thought as Susanna came out of the café carrying that cute little baby of hers.

"Is it fixed?" she asked, strolling across the street, her rumpled pale yellow dress caressing her gentle curves as she moved. She had a firm, willowy body. She looked fresh, untouched, and there was something about her that made a man ache to worship her skin, to stroke her gently as if he was going to teach her something solemn and beautiful and momentous when she had clearly known a man's touch many times. That baby hadn't sprouted from the ground, and it looked enough like her for him to know there were blood ties. She couldn't really be innocent, but there was an unmarred eagerness she exuded that called up the protective warrior in him…

Brady nearly swore.

"It's done," he said, and he knew that he was talking about more than her car.

She reached him, looked down and started digging in her purse. "I don't know how much the parts cost," she said, suddenly gazing up at him.

He wanted to tell her that it didn't matter, that she wasn't going to pay him, but as if she read his intent, she firmed her chin and frowned. "We'll call it an even hundred," he said, giving in. "You'll pay me later when you've had time to find a place and when we settle up on the rent." There, that should soothe her.

But she had a suspicious look in her eyes. "You're not trying to put something past me, are you?" she asked.

"I'm a truthful man, Susanna," he said and he wasn't lying. It was one good thing he could say about himself, but then even that was a bit of a lie, because there were sins of omission that were as bad or worse than lies, and he had been guilty of that kind of sin several times over in his life. Serious sins of omission, too. Times when he had known what he was doing and had gone ahead and done the wrong thing anyway.

"I trust you," she said softly, taking her hand from her purse.

"Don't," he said, but he didn't bother to explain himself. She didn't ask for an explanation. He handed her the keys, eager to finally be gone from this place where he had known plenty of bad times. As his fingers touched hers, he braced himself for his first personal contact with her. Her skin was softer than he'd imagined, but then he hadn't allowed himself to imagine much.

Brady took a step back and turned toward his own car. "You remember the way?" he asked, but at that moment he looked up and straight into the eyes of the one man he didn't want to meet ever again in his life.

Lon Banks was in his early thirties, an attorney. But once he had been the pride of Red Rose, a young and promising baseball star with a good shot at a college scholarship and maybe even the majors…until Brady's brother, Frank, drunk and driving too fast, had mowed Lon down and left him bleeding in the street. Brady had been thirteen. Brady's father and Frank had threatened to beat him to death if he snitched. They'd beat him before, badly, many times, but never almost to death. And so he'd never told what he knew, and it was only due to a passing motorist who had been able to identify Frank's car that his brother had been put behind bars.

That was thirteen years ago. Brady's father and Frank were long gone, drowning when they got drunk and tipped their boat over. And Brady had been a victim of an auto accident himself, but that had been his own fault. Lon was blameless. The accident had ruined his arm and killed his hopes of baseball fame.

And when Lon looked at Brady, Brady knew that the truth was there between them. A Malone had taken Lon Banks's dreams, and there was still one guilty Malone to remind him of the fact from time to time.

Lon passed by without either of them speaking.

"Brady?" Susanna asked, the concern in her voice apparent. He wanted to tell her not to worry for him. He was the guilty party here. He had kept his brother's secret, he had not stopped his best friend, Davis, from driving that military vehicle, even though he should have been aware that Davis had had too much to drink. Both accidents had cost dearly; Lon's hopes, Davis's life, his own budding career in the army, the only life where he had ever felt he fit. But it was right that he should suffer, because he was the one who had been at fault. And there was no justification for Susanna wasting her concern on someone like him. He had taken the easy way out—twice—and worlds had shattered. The Malones had always had bad reputations, and he had done nothing to re-write history.

"Brady?" Susanna asked again, and he could tell by her tone that he was making her nervous.

Brady shook his head suddenly as if to shake off his mood. "The car's ready to roll. Let's go. I'll get you fitted out at the…well, for lack of a better term, let's just call it the guest house," he said, struggling to push the ghosts away and to lighten his voice. None of this, after all, had anything to do with this fragile woman. And none of it was her fault. He didn't want her to be touched by his darkness. Actually, he didn't want anything to do with her at all, but then he was the idiot who had been unable to stop himself from driving into town and offering to fix her car and to put her up at his place.

There were consequences for everything, and didn't he know that all too well?

"I'll be right behind you," Susanna said.

"If you remember the way, you'll be right in front of me. I want to see how that car is running."

She nodded, and soon they were both on the road. Brady was soon satisfied that her car was going to be all right, and he began to take note of the scenery. He wondered what rural Red Rose would look like to a stranger used to living in a city like Chicago. He especially wondered what was going through Susanna's head when they passed Sunny Delavan's Big Babe Dairy Shop with its twenty-foot high statue of a big-busted woman wearing a tight red dress. Most of the people of Red Rose had developed a fondness for the statue, partially because they liked Sunny Delavan, but he was sure that there were outsiders who simply considered the statue tacky and were embarrassed by it. He would imagine that there was a lot about Red Rose that would take some getting used to for a city girl like Susanna. The emptiness of his own land, for instance.

But when she climbed out of her car and circled around to pull her baby into her arms, Susanna was smiling.

"Everything is so fresh here," she said. "And open and free. It's as if you can do and be anything." For a minute he thought she was going to spin around in a circle with her arms out. Maybe she would have, if she hadn't been holding a baby.

And she was wrong, so very wrong. "This is a small town," he reminded her. "Everyone knows everyone else's business most of the time. Some people find that more restrictive than living in a city.''

As if he'd doused a candle, she lost her smile. ''I suppose you're right. Everyone has things they'd prefer that others didn't know about themselves.'' Her voice was low, strained, and he felt as if he'd just kicked a kitten.

''But everyone here knows the good things, too. Nobody has to toot their own whistle. Just do a good deed, and see if you don't get a hundred pats on the back before the week is out.'' Not that he knew that from personal experience, but he was pretty sure that Susanna was the kind who did good deeds. It would be true for her.

''Are you trying to make me feel better?'' she asked, studying him from beneath half-lowered lashes. And his heart began to clatter heavily, his hands felt big and sweaty, his body felt strained and awkward.

Brady turned away. ''I'd better go see what shape your home is in,'' he said thickly.

She followed closely on his heels. She was there when he opened the creaky door of the building that had once been a garage with an attached shed lean-to, and that he had converted into living space when he had been a rebellious teenager seeking solitude. He had even dug a line from the house and added some creaking plumbing to turn the shed into something resembling a bath, barely serviceable but there.

Sunlight streamed into the small space through the door and two windows on one side. It revealed bare wood walls that he had once covered in blankets and posters, a naked light bulb hanging from the ceiling, a concrete floor on which he had thrown an almost-room-size piece of navy-blue carpeting that someone had discarded. Its edges were ragged.

A sagging tan-colored couch sat against one wall, a chipped wooden table with one leg shorter than the rest graced another. Several mismatched kitchen chairs, most of which had padding protruding from the ripped vinyl seats, were scattered around the room, along with a battered wooden trunk, a small bookcase and an old double bed. The mattress was still good. It was the only thing he'd bought new, because he had hoped to get lucky with Samantha Dodge, and a good bed had seemed a prerequisite for such a momentous event, even to an awkward teenage boy.

Dust covered everything. The room, on the whole, was a disaster. Fine for a sixteen-year-old boy, eager for independence. All wrong for a grown woman with a baby.

For half a second Brady felt like a teenage boy again. Embarrassment and anger flooded through him. But he forced himself to turn to Susanna.

"Tonight you get my house. This place is a pit. You can't stay here."

Immediately her eyes went all soft and distressed. She held out one hand as if to touch his arm to stop him from saying any more, but then she hastily pulled back. "Stay in your house? No, this is fine."

He eyed the room again. "It's a dive, Susanna. I haven't been in here for a while. I'd forgotten what it looked like."

"It's fine. Really. It just needs some cleaning and straightening."

Her voice had risen a bit, as if the strain of trying to convince him was almost too much. "It doesn't even have finished walls," he said. "At least take my room for one night."

She shook her head vehemently. "No, I don't want to…to stay in a man's house."

And something kindled inside of him, a hint of suspicion, the kind that made a man deeply angry. He remembered how she had looked the first moment he'd seen her, the fear in her eyes. Someone had scared her once. Badly.

"I'll give you the key. You can lock me out."

"Sometimes locks don't work."

He started to say that he would give his word, but then…he knew what his word was worth.

"I like it here," she said suddenly. "It's small and convenient and uncomplicated. Uncomplicated is good," she explained, and then she turned that earnest look on him again. "Brady, I don't have anywhere else to go, but I really don't want to go to your house. It's not that I don't trust you. I just… I just need to be as independent as I can, as unobtrusive. This feels all right. Staying in your house doesn't."

He didn't answer at first. It wasn't right for a woman who looked like her and one who had a small child to boot to be staying in a hovel like this.

"This place will make it easier," she said, still trying to convince him.

"Make what easier?"

"Being here. Being dependent. I came to Red Rose on a quest to be free of all the restrictions life has imposed on me."

And now he understood. He'd been trying to kick free of the restrictions of his world all his life.

"So Red Rose is living up to your expectations?"

She smiled again, a gentle smile that made him want to lean close and taste her smile with his tongue.

"It's a good place to rest," she agreed.

"And when you're done resting?"

She shrugged.

"You fly away like a bird?" A bird flushed from its nest like a pheasant, he was guessing, judging by the look of discomfort on her face.

"Forget I asked that. As you said before, we all have things we don't want to share with the world," he said. "What you do with your life here and your future elsewhere is your business and no one else's." He knew that better than anyone.

Her eyes glowed with satisfaction. "I got a job," she declared.

He raised one brow. "So soon? Where?"

"At the café. I'm taking Ellie Donahue's waitress job."

A waitress. Brady couldn't help glancing down at Susanna's yellow dress. It was rumpled, but clearly expensive. He knew that much. He very much doubted that she had ever done that kind of labor in her life. She looked as if she had been raised to grace a tea table or to lead a man into a waltz at a ball. But he refused to ask any questions about her past, not when she so clearly didn't want to talk about it.

"What will you do with the baby?"

"Lydia says I can bring her with me."

He nodded. "I'm sure you'll be a fine waitress."

She took a deep breath. "I want to be. It seems silly, somehow, but it's important that I be the very best waitress I can be. It matters to me to be good at something. I want Grace to grow up knowing that a person should try his or her utmost to do the best job possible, no matter what the job is.''

Brady glanced down at the sleeping baby. "She looks to be very good at sleeping," he mused.

Susanna laughed, a pretty sound in the stillness. "She's a total expert on that field. And on gurgling and playing with her toes. She's such a good baby."

And it was obvious that Susanna loved her to death. She was a caring mother. Somehow that made Brady realize that they really did come from different worlds. Only circumstance and chance had thrown them together for this short while. Standing here, gazing down at this pretty, fragile woman with her eyes that lit up at the thought of taking on a simple job many people would have turned down, something dangerous stirred in Brady, and he had to get away.

"I'd better go see if I can find someplace for her to sleep," he said. "There's probably an old bassinet or cradle in the barn. Maybe more than one. It's full of relics, and surely there's something that will be serviceable for tonight. I'll get sheets and blankets and something for you to eat. A broom, too."

He turned to go, but as he did, she placed her hand on his arm. A light touch, barely skin-to-skin contact at all, but it stopped him as effectively as a brick wall rising in his path.

"Thank you," she said. "This wasn't exactly how I anticipated this day would go. Lots of bad and unexpected things happening. Thank you for making it easier for me."

Brady wanted to swear. Could she really not see what this place looked like? Did she really think he would have gone into town to help her today if he didn't hate Nate Fisher to the core? He didn't know what her thoughts were, but he knew that his own motives weren't pure. He'd seen a situation and he'd reacted to it. There was nothing noble in his actions, and there never had been.

He nodded, acknowledging her gratitude but unable to say so in words. After all, what had he done? "I'll put out feelers, tomorrow," he said instead. "Maybe someone has a nice room they'll rent you," he said.

"Yes," she said softly. "Then you and Scrap can get back to your work, and Grace and I can move on the way we intended to in the first place."

That would be best, he thought. If she moved on quickly. Because as she removed her fingers from his arm, he had a terrible urge to turn and slide his fingertips down her cheek, to touch her, to see if her eyes went all soft and dreamy the way they had earlier in the day.

That wasn't his way. After years of straining to catch things and hold on to them, he had learned to let anything he wanted slide through his fingers like water. Never staying, never catching, never really mattering. It was a good way to be. It saved him a lot of trouble and stress down the road.

He didn't like stress, and he'd seen his share. He was sure Susanna had seen more than her share, too. He didn't intend to be the cause of more trouble in her life.

But as he left the pile of supplies inside the door of her temporary home, his gaze met hers once, her eyes soft and green and grateful. The warmth of her expression slipped through his skin and traveled all the way to his toes. Instant heat claimed him as he noticed the gentle curve of her lips.

"Good night," Brady said roughly, determined to

move away quickly and stop thinking about laying Susanna Wright down and kissing her. He turned to go, then on impulse turned back. "If you want Scrap to stay with you, I'll send him over. He's an excellent watchdog."

Those pretty pink lips curved up just a touch. "I remember. But you might need him for companionship and I think we'll be fine. I'm not really afraid of raccoons, and I don't think anyone will find me tonight."

Brady nodded and frowned slightly. Susanna's eyes widened a touch. She bit her lip, and for a second he thought she was going to amend her comment, but she probably knew as well as he did that trying to take back something once said only made things worse. No matter. He wasn't going to question what she'd meant.

At least not out loud. What he'd thought before was true, then. Susanna Wright was on the run. And all that stood between her and the someone looking for her was him.

Outside of his job in the service, he had never been a protector. He didn't know who she was running from. Someone bad or someone good.

It didn't matter. Whoever they were, they weren't going to get her without getting past him.

Chapter Four

"How did things go between you and Brady last night?" Sunny Delavan asked the next day as Susanna poured the woman her first cup of coffee.

Susanna hoped she wasn't blushing as she remembered waking up in the middle of the night and looking out her window, staring toward Brady's house. His lights had been off. She wondered if he was sleeping and what he looked like when he slept. Did his stern face relax? Did he dream? The thought of him stretching that big muscular body in his sleep had made her take a deep breath. She'd pressed her legs close together and tried to blot out the image of Brady half-naked or even all naked beneath the covers.

Sleep had been a mere memory after that. It had not been the right kind of beginning to her relationship with her landlord.

"Things went just fine," she said airily, hoping that a bolt of lightning wouldn't snake out of the clear blue sky and strike her down.

"Don't ever play poker, sweetie," Sunny told her with an amused glance.

"I'm sure things went fine, Sunny," a thin woman wearing a high-necked ruffled blouse said. "Mr. Malone has always been most polite to me."

"I know that, Tommy. I was referring to the fact that he might be a man who could get under a woman's skin," Sunny said gently.

"Oh, his sexual appeal," Tommy said in a voice that indicated that she knew just what she was talking about even though her appearance shouted the word *virgin*. "Yes, he's very well proportioned, I do believe. Not that I'm talking in anything but a purely professional manner, you understand."

"Thomasina is a professional matchmaker," Lydia explained to Susanna.

Susanna blinked. "Well, I hardly… I don't think… Brady—"

Tommy waved her hand in dismissal. "Oh, don't worry, Susanna. I only match people up who want to be matched up. Brady, unfortunately, doesn't." She sighed. "He told me so in no uncertain times the only time I dared ring his doorbell to ask. He was most convincing. That man can certainly glower."

Susanna knew just what Tommy meant, but still, this was one part of Brady that she understood. "Not everyone wants to be married," she said softly.

And when Tommy stared into her eyes, the woman saw too much. Susanna swiftly looked away.

"Oh, well, I'd better be going," the matchmaker said. "I have a date tonight," she announced to the small breakfast crowd.

"With a man?" Joyce Hives asked, her voice teasing.

Tommy blinked. "Yes," she said. "Very definitely, yes. A real date with a real man."

"Jeff Seaton?" Sunny guessed.

"How did you know?" Tommy asked, her face turning pink.

Sunny shrugged, a wide grin on her face. "Honey, I know when a man wants a woman. Besides, every time he gets near you, Jeff tries to look down your blouse."

Tommy pressed her hand over her fully covered bosom. "It's so embarrassing," she agreed, but there was a note of something else in her voice. Excitement, Susanna thought. "Do you think I'm wrong to go out with him?" Tommy asked. "I'm not...well, I'm sure you know that I've hardly ever been on a date in my life, and he has a reputation for being a bit wild. Should I have told him no?"

Sunny blew out a big breath that lifted her bangs. "Honey, I am the last person to give advice. I love men, but I've just spent weeks running from Chester, only to finally figure out that he is the man made for me. I used to think I knew it all where men were concerned, but not anymore. Anyone else here have any advice for Tommy? You, Susanna?"

Susanna shook her head vehemently. "I make bad choices where men are concerned. I would never give advice to any woman concerning affairs of the heart. Besides, I don't want to get married ever again."

"Sounds like you and Brady are a pair then," Sunny announced, and that was all it took to shake Susanna up. She barely managed to keep the pot from wobbling as she poured her next cup of coffee.

"Brady is my landlord," she said, "and that's all."

Her voice quivered slightly even though she tried to keep it still.

"That's okay, honey," Sunny said soothingly. "Sometimes…well, most times, I just have a big mouth and I say things I shouldn't. At least not until you know me well enough to know that I'm just teasing. Still, I suppose Brady isn't the kind of man a person should tease about. He's got some dark moments in his past."

Susanna plunked down her pot of coffee. She thought of Trent and all the dark moments he'd brought to her life. She reminded herself that she had Grace to worry about, and she had no business inviting any darkness into her daughter's life. "What do you mean by dark?"

Lydia shook her head at Sunny. "We don't really know all of Brady's secrets. I'm sure you realize that he's not the kind of man to share. But he grew up with a father who was as mean as they come and a brother who was almost as mean and twice as irresponsible. And Brady got into trouble with the law now and then, too. Drinking, fighting, that kind of thing. He had a mountain-size chip on his shoulder. We all figured he would self-destruct sooner or later, and he was well on the way to doing that when a judge told him that he could choose jail or the military. Brady went into the army and began to turn himself around. He found something he excelled at, and then there was some sort of a car accident. That was the end of his promising military career. That's all I know about Brady's dark side. I'm sure there's more to it than that, much more. But he doesn't hand out the details, and I wouldn't expect him to. He's the kind of man who could hurt a woman just by being himself.'' She gave Susanna a kind look, but one that warned her to be careful nonetheless.

Susanna took a deep breath. She looked at her employer. "I am the most careful woman you'll ever meet, Lydia," she said. Then she forced another smile. "Now who needs a fortifying cup of coffee?"

She had the most awful feeling that *she* needed fortifying more than anyone in the room, however. What Lydia had just told her about Brady made her realize just how careful she needed to be. If she didn't watch herself, she'd turn into one of those sad pathetic creatures who kept making the same mistakes with men.

"Not going to happen," she said with a frown.

"What?"

Susanna blinked. She looked down to see that Delia Sable was holding her coffee cup out to be filled.

"Sorry," Susanna said, and she poured the cup of coffee.

So Brady had seen his dreams crushed just as she had. And he was a very private person. That hadn't stopped him from helping a woman and child in need. No question, Brady Malone was a very deep individual.

He was obviously a man she would be a fool to get too close to.

But darn it, she owed him a favor or two.

Brady was putting out food for Scrap when there was a knock on the door. He knew who it was. He'd been instantly aware when Susanna had driven onto the property after spending the day at the Red Rose. He had forced himself to avoid looking her way.

But now the woman was on his front porch. What was a man to do?

He rose and went to the door, pulling on the old brass knob. "Yes?" he asked, standing in the doorway. He supposed a more polite man, a more civilized man, a different kind of man would invite her in. But he took one look at that clean pretty hair, those deep green eyes and the eager smile and knew that there was no way he could have her in his house.

And he couldn't have that little blue-eyed cherub in here, either. This was strictly male territory, and he was the only male who entered here anymore. Except for Scrap.

"I finished my first day at work," Susanna said. She tried to peer past him. He barely held back a smile, but he crossed his arms, letting her know that, bad manners or no, he was not budging and inviting her into his house.

Brady nodded. "Good. You look like you survived."

She wrinkled her nose and adjusted her baby more snugly on her hip. "Everyone was very patient with me, even when I spilled coffee right on Sunny Delavan's chest."

Her tone sounded mortified. Brady struggled to keep from laughing. "Um, yeah, well, Sunny certainly has...a chest." Sunny was a big woman in every way.

"I thought I was aiming for the cup. I didn't realize that it was just slightly beneath...well, anyway, she was really nice about it. She said she'd get her boyfriend, Chester, to lick her clean."

As the words left her lips, Susanna clapped a hand over her mouth, her eyes oh-no-what-have-I-said wide above her hand. The hot pink color surged up her throat and tinted all the lovely skin Brady could see. He had a sudden urge to lick something on Susanna, she looked that distraught and delicious.

Brady took a step back, as if that would keep his salacious thoughts at bay.

"I know," she said, staring at the space that now stood between them. "I can't believe I repeated that, either."

He finally couldn't help smiling. "I don't think Sunny would mind. I always got the feeling that she liked being a little outrageous. She'd probably be happy that you were helping her reputation along by repeating her comments."

Susanna still looked a bit uncomfortable. She slowly lowered her hand and nodded. Silence bloomed between them.

"Was there anything you needed?" Brady asked. "Some problem with the car or the…building?" He looked across at the wreck of a hut she was living in. No one would call that thing a home. Surely she would find something more suitable soon, and then he could stop thinking about her.

"I just wanted to pay you for the next week," she said with a hard nod. "Lydia gave me an advance, and I wanted to start settling my debts right away." She held out a handful of bills. Brady didn't reach out. He looked at the shack again.

"Forget it," he said.

And then the lovely lady got a mean, stubborn look in her eyes. "I pay my way," she said. "I don't take charity."

"That," he said, gesturing toward the shack, "would never be called charity by any man."

She leaned into his space, her body half in his doorway now. "It kept the cool air away from Grace and me last night. It keeps the bugs out, and I can fix it up a little if I need to. *And*," she added, "you can't tell me that you didn't go easy on me with the car. I want to pay."

He narrowed his eyes and stepped forward, purposely trying to intimidate. It was a technique he had learned at a very young age, and it had always worked in the past, especially in the military. His size and his demeanor alone were usually enough to make other men back off.

Susanna visibly swallowed, but she didn't scurry away. "Please," she said, her voice strained. "I need to. I need to be in control of my life."

And he suddenly wanted to curse, to hit something. She had said the one thing he couldn't argue with, he who had spent his whole life seeking the control that had so often been denied him.

He reached out and snatched one bill from her grasp, his fingers just barely touching hers, but the sensation of her skin against his sent heat pouring through his body, turning his blood molten, his groin heavy, his thoughts forbidden.

"You said ten a night. That's only twenty dollars for the whole week," she protested, her voice a shaky whisper.

"That's all any man could ask for the rental of what is, essentially, a garage," he said.

"It's my home," she insisted.

"When you're gone, I'll store auto parts and junk there," he retaliated. "It's not worth more than twenty. Take it or leave it." He didn't find the fact amusing that normally it would be the buyer who would say such a thing. Enticing as she was, he didn't want to start something with Susanna that would have her struggling long-term to pay back a perceived debt to him. He didn't want to think of anything long-term where this woman was concerned.

"Twenty and that's all," he repeated.

She slowly raised her chin. "All right, Brady," she said. "That's what you'll get." And she turned and walked away, Gracie smiling over her shoulder. He could almost have sworn that she'd said the words, "For now." But that was probably just his imagination. What woman would insist on paying more than something was worth when he had made it clear that he didn't want anything from her?

And for damn sure she didn't want anything from him. The darn woman wouldn't even accept the loan of a hovel from him. Not that that was so unusual. The people of Red Rose were smart enough to know that they couldn't trust a Malone. Things had always been uneasy between him and the town.

And now things were uneasy between him and Susanna Wright. That shouldn't have bothered him, but he awakened in the night with a deep ache in both his body and soul.

He sat up in bed and heard the telltale sound of rain on the roof. He heard a car door slam and looked out the window.

Susanna was placing Grace in the car. She got in beside her baby and tucked a blanket around her child. She shoved a pillow beneath her own head.

The darn building must be leaking. Brady swore long and loud, loud enough that Scrap raised his head and looked at his master accusingly.

"Okay, that wasn't very nice," Brady admitted,

"but what am I supposed to do? Invite them in here?"

Scrap gazed at him soulfully.

Brady frowned. "You are just too softhearted," he told his dog, but he threw on his jeans, rammed his feet in his boots and slogged out to Susanna's car. He rapped on the window.

She rolled it down an inch.

"Come on inside," he told her. "You can't be comfortable here."

She shook her head. "I'm beginning to feel like a walking disaster. You can't keep rescuing me. I can't keep letting you do that. I don't like leaning on people. I like doing for myself, taking care of my baby alone. I appreciate your generosity, but we're fine."

"You're wet," he pointed out. "And this will be the second night that you've slept in your car. Tomorrow you have a full day of standing on your feet. Come inside. I have two spare rooms. They both have solid locks."

"It's not that I don't trust you," she said suddenly.

"Well, that doesn't say too much for your judgment," he argued. "You shouldn't trust me, but as I said, the doors lock tight."

She hesitated, biting her lip. He wondered if she knew just how much that gesture made a man want to throw open the door to her car, let the floodgates to his greed open and kiss her crazy.

He forced himself to breathe slowly, fighting the ragged hunger that surged within him. "Susanna, I don't know if you've noticed, but I'm getting wet."

And that was all it took. "All right, we'll come inside, but just for tonight," she said. "Tomorrow I'll get someone to take care of the leaks in my place."

Her place. It sounded so permanent. It was the completely wrong word for such a dump, and she said it with such pride. For the first time Brady allowed himself to wonder just what she'd come from to make her so grateful for such little things.

His heart felt full at the thought, his throat started to close off. He grunted to cover up his confusion.

"Don't be a bear," Susanna told him. "I said I'd stay in your house tonight. Are you happy now?"

Was he happy? Knowing that a woman with lips like pink candy and a tight little feminine body was going to be only two rooms away? A woman who was completely off-limits if he wanted to hang on to what little self-respect he still possessed?

Dammit no, he wasn't happy.

He was on fire and had been ever since she arrived in town. He wished to hell that Susanna could go back to wherever she had come from.

But he knew somehow that she never could.

Something or someone was after her, and he, ineffectual and useless as he was, was all that stood between her and her pursuers right now.

Heaven help the woman. She was in big trouble.

When Susanna stepped into her home the next day after work, she breathed in the scent of newly cut wood. Immediately she looked up and saw that the holes in the roof had been covered. Several boxes sat inside the door and, placing Grace on a blanket with her favorite ring of plastic keys, Susanna went over to one of the boxes, knelt in front of it and peeled back the cardboard flaps.

Inside was an assortment of blue and white dishes, a small microwave, a hot plate and an exquisite crystal vase. The second box contained towels to hang in the small primitive bathroom attached to the building, extra sheets, a baby monitor, candles and matches. At the bottom of the box lay a white teddy bear wrapped in plastic. It looked new. It didn't look like the kind of thing a man might find lying around his attic.

For a second, tears pricked the back of Susanna's eyes, her throat felt raw and full. She blinked hard and picked up the bear, pulling back its plastic covering. It was softer than rabbit's fur, and she pressed it to her face. "Grace, that man…well, we just have to do something to thank him. I know darn well from what everyone has said that he doesn't like going into town, but I'm pretty sure he didn't pick this up just anywhere, and this—" she pointed to the vase that she had removed from the box "—this is not the kind of thing that a callous man would have thought of. He's been good to us. Better than good. If he hadn't let us stay here and fixed our car and now…helped us this way, we would be a lot worse off. We might even be eating out of Dumpsters. What do you think we can do to repay him when he won't take money?"

Grace looked at her with big blue eyes and blinked. She held up her keys and rattled them, cooing.

"Yes, sweetie, we have to give him something, too, but what?"

Grace wrinkled her nose and then laughed. It was very cute, but not much help.

Susanna looked in the direction of Brady's house. She wondered what he did over there all alone. It was obvious that he hadn't wanted to let her in his house last night, but he had refused to let her sleep in her car again. Consequently, as soon as he had shown her and Grace to the spare room, he had completely disappeared into the other end of the rambling ranch house. This morning he had left food out for her, but Brady himself had been nowhere in sight.

His house had been neat and clean but rather spartan. She assumed he did his own cooking and cleaning. He wouldn't want anyone invading his space.

But did a person necessarily have to invade his space to offer him a proper thank-you?

Surely there was another way, and her day job gave her access to a lot of women who, no doubt, had had experience with a lot of men over the years.

There was no way Brady was going to walk away without a proper thank-you, and Susanna was counting on the ladies of Red Rose to help her think of a way to get past his defenses.

Chapter Five

"Pie. Definitely pie," Joyce Hives announced the next morning.

"No, hon. I'd say cake. A big, fat, chocolate layer cake," Sunny countered.

Susanna's confidence fell. "Baking? You think I should bake him something?"

"Way to a man's heart," Lydia said.

"I don't want to know how to reach his heart," Susanna said faintly. "I certainly don't want him to think I'm pursuing him."

"Hon, it's just food, and that was just an expression Lydia here was using," Sunny pointed out.

"I know. It's just— I was never a really good baker. The basics of cooking, but baking is so…exact, so unforgiving. A pie crust that isn't tough as nails? A cake where the frosting won't slide off the top?" She frowned and bit her lip, trying not to remember her baking disasters or the way Trent had ridiculed her attempts and gotten angry when things hadn't gone right.

The women sitting at the tables exchanged several glances. "Brownies are easy," Joyce offered.

"And they're chocolate," Rosellen January noted.

"Everyone likes brownies," Mercy Granahan added.

"And I've got just the recipe," Lydia said, patting Susanna's shoulder. "Even Grace here could manage it, and I guarantee it will bring tears to the man's eyes. He'll look at you in a wholly different light. He'll be your slave for life after one bite."

A vision of Brady with those sexy dark blue eyes looking at her in a whole new light made Susanna swallow hard. She probably shouldn't even go there. "I just want to thank the man, since he won't take my money," she said hoarsely.

"Well then, put that coffeepot down," Lydia said decisively, "and let's get you into the kitchen. Brady Malone is about to be thanked in a way his taste buds will never forget."

Brady was at the back of the house chopping wood later that afternoon when he heard Susanna drive up. He had been sitting at his desk for hours trying to concentrate on work and ignoring his memory of the breathy thank-you Susanna had given him yesterday as she'd stood in front of him clutching the white teddy bear.

"This is too much," she had said, cradling the bear against her breast. And staring into her clear green eyes, he had had to agree that she was right. Everything about his reaction to the woman was just too much. And so, when it had become obvious that he wasn't going to get any work done, he had done the only thing a man could do in such a circumstance; he had gone outside to beat on an inanimate object. The chunks of wood flew as he applied the ax with all the strength he could muster.

If he made enough noise and pushed himself hard enough, he wouldn't hear her going about her evening's activities. He could exhaust himself and finally sleep. And tomorrow he would be rested enough to work.

But eventually he ran out of wood. He picked up his shirt and draped it over his sweat-soaked shoulder. Rounding the house, he saw a small something balanced on the railing of his porch.

He moved closer and saw a plate of brownies on a blue glass plate.

"The plate is Lydia's. She loaned it to me." Susanna's soft voice came from behind him. He turned to see her standing in the doorway of the garage.

"Brownies?"

"You wouldn't take money. You don't like brownies?" Her voice sounded uncertain. "If you don't—"

He held up one hand. "You made those?"

"I had some help. A lot of help." A smile lifted her lips, making her look pretty and fresh as she moved across the yard and up to where he was standing. "But mostly I made them."

And the pride in her voice was so childlike, so uncontainable, that he couldn't tell her what he wanted to tell her, to stop trying to pay a debt she didn't owe.

"They look good," he said instead, shifting a bit awkwardly, running a hand over his bare chest.

Her gaze dropped to where his hand was moving.

Her eyes widened and she quickly looked up. "Lydia says that no man has ever resisted them, that she's had men almost cry after eating just one bite. I think I'll just be happy if you manage to keep down the first bite. I have to tell you that even with help, I'm not too confident that these will be all that good. I'm not real experienced in the field of baking."

And what could he do? He walked over to the plate, picked up a brownie and took a big bite. A little dry, a bit uneven, but watching Susanna twist her hands beneath her breasts as she waited for his verdict, he could predict that a man would do many things just to have this woman standing this close and looking as if his opinion mattered.

"Delicious," he said.

She raised one brow. "I'll get better," she promised in a voice that almost made him cry, just as Lydia had predicted.

"Don't," he said softly. "Don't get better. These are good." And they were. They were tasting better with every bite. "Thank you. Are we even now?"

She smiled then, a smile that promised something he didn't want to know what. "Not yet," she said. "A plate of brownies can't make up for what you've done for me." And then Brady truly did want to cry. She was going to continue to pester him, to insist she owed him something. Maybe he should have just taken her money. It was what his father would have done. His brother, too.

He picked up the plate of brownies. "I can share," he said, trying to let her know that she was done paying him.

"I already had one," she said.

"The baby?" He looked around her to where

Grace was playing in the yard in a playpen he had found.

"The baby shouldn't have brownies. You've been good to her."

"Who wouldn't be? She's a baby."

But when he looked at Susanna, her eyes were dark and troubled. She no longer looked as if she wanted to be near him.

"I have to go inside now," she said, and she scurried to Grace, picked her up and swept into the garage, clicking the door tight behind her.

Brady took a deep breath. He carried the plate of brownies inside. Scrap lay on the hearth.

"The lady made me brownies," he told his dog. "The lady has been mistreated by someone, and she's still pretty scared about that. What are we going to do about that, boy?"

Scrap didn't answer, giving Brady that patient, soulful look. But it didn't matter. Brady knew what he was going to do. He turned to his computer, clicked on to his favorite search engine and typed in Susanna's name.

Susanna placed Grace in her car seat. She placed a kiss on her daughter's forehead, breathing in the sweet baby scent of her.

"Stay here, sweetie. Mom will be right back. We have to go wash our clothes."

Grace blew a bubble and giggled.

"Hmm, wish I thought doing laundry was that much fun," Susanna said as she turned and went to pick up the basket of laundry she'd left just inside the door. She had balanced it on her hip and was just turning to carry it to the car when Brady stepped into her path.

"What are you doing?"

She tipped up her basket. "Have to have clean clothes. I'm down to my last blouse. One drop of coffee on this and I'm lost," she said, looking down at the expanse of white that covered her chest.

"You're not going to the Suds 'N' Stuff over in Hightrail?"

"I've been informed that it's the only place around."

"It's a place where punk out-of-work men like to drink and pick up lonely women doing their wash."

She leveled a killing look at him. "I'm pretty sure I can resist the lures of a drunken male propositioning me."

"It's not a nice place."

"Does it have washing machines?"

"Of course."

"Then I don't have any choice. I refuse to use a dishpan and beat my clothes against a rock."

"I have a machine."

Susanna blinked. Brady had frowned when he'd said that last. She knew he didn't like her invading his space. He didn't really like having her here at all, she was pretty sure. But he was standing here with those muscular arms crossed, daring her to turn down his offer.

"Well, you don't look drunk," she finally said. "And I'll bet I won't have to have a supply of quarters, either."

He visibly relaxed. Slightly.

"Come on, I'll show you the way," he said.

But she stood her ground. "I'll use your washer on

one condition." Would you listen to me? she thought. The man is offering me the chance to avoid driving out of my way to a place that sounds as if the police visit it regularly and I'm making conditions? Still, she remained firm, not budging, lifting her chin as if daring him to say what she had just thought.

"What's the condition?" His voice was low, gravelly, the kind of voice a woman dreamed of in her bedroom. She wondered how many women had built erotic fantasies around Brady whispering to them in the shadows.

She took a deep breath and tried to concentrate on what he had asked her.

"I'll use your machine if you let me wash your things, too."

He opened his mouth. To protest, she was sure.

"It's only fair," she quickly added.

"Fair has never been something I've counted on," he said. "I don't intend to start now."

There was something unreadable in his voice. The remnants of pain? She remembered what the women in the Red Rose Café had told her about his upbringing, but she figured that he wouldn't want to give her the details of his life. He could obviously barely stand to be near her. "I believe in fairness," she said suddenly, "and I have to live with myself. If you won't let me repay you in the only way I can, then I'll just have to turn down your kind offer. I'm not really afraid of what's going to happen to me in a Laundromat in broad daylight." She started to turn back to her car.

Suddenly her basket was removed from her hands. She turned angry eyes on Brady.

"You win," he said.

"What?" That wasn't a phrase she had heard from a man, at least not in recent times.

"You win. You can wash my damn clothes. I'll just carry these in for you." And he walked away, his limp a bit more pronounced today, his back stiff and proud as he moved in front of her.

When he disappeared into his house with her basket of dirty clothing, Susanna turned to Grace. "I don't think he's real happy with me right now, sweetie."

Grace's babbling response seemed to agree.

"Well, let's get to this," Susanna said. She walked up to Brady's door and let herself in. She wasn't quite sure where exactly he had gone so she started toward the back of the house. There in a small room with sunshine streaming in windows that bordered three sides was the most up-to-date washer and dryer Susanna had ever seen. On top of the washer was her basket of clothes along with detergent and fabric softener. Next to the washer on the floor was the basket of Brady's clothes.

The man was nowhere in sight.

Susanna kissed the top of Grace's head. "He sure works fast, doesn't he, pumpkin? Guess it's pretty obvious he doesn't want us around, though."

She was just about to find a place on the floor for Grace to play when Brady appeared in the doorway. He was carrying the playpen in one hand and a bag in the other. He put down the bag and quickly snapped the playpen into position, putting it out of reach of anything dangerous. Then he dug into the bag and pulled out a brightly colored musical bird toy and hung it over the side of the playpen. Susanna had seen the bright yellow birds in the stores. They were motion-operated and very expensive.

"Brady," she said. "I— Thank you. You are, without a doubt, the nicest man I've met in years."

For a minute he stared at her, his blue eyes fierce. His gaze dropped from her eyes to her lips.

She had an almost overwhelming urge to lick them or to step close to him and touch, to ask him to touch her the way she had once thought she wanted to be touched. Instead she forced herself to hold still. "Thank you," she said again, faintly.

He stared at her some more. "What kind of man was he?" he asked suddenly.

"Who?" she asked, but she knew who he meant.

"Your husband."

Susanna took a deep breath and forced her thoughts away from the man in front of her. She made herself think of the man who she had been married to for three years. "I thought he was a good man once," she said.

"Exactly," Brady said, and he turned and walked away. She knew he wouldn't be coming back to this part of the house until she was gone.

Brady sat staring at his computer screen as if he was actually going to get any work done with Susanna and baby Grace in his house. This building…it was old, but he had thrown himself into altering the interior. He had tried thus to chase away the old bad memories, but no matter how many new appliances he added, the house still remained the same to him in many ways. And in time, he had decided that was a good thing. It reminded him to never forget the past, to never forget who and what he was, and he was okay with that. Almost content.

But now…

"She's humming," he whispered to himself. "Some off-key thing that's..." Sweet, he thought. Charming. Susanna Wright was oblivious to the darkness that pervaded his house. She didn't know his past, didn't know his family's stories, and here in this place where bad memories had been made, she was humming to her heart's content, bringing a light to the place that had never existed before. Even though he was sure some very bad dark things had happened to her, she could still hum as if her world were filled with sunshine.

Brady marveled at that.

Then she started to sing softly. He strained to hear the words, but he couldn't quite make them all out. Still, her tone implied enough. The general gist was that life was beautiful, fun, promising and filled with love and good things.

"She's singing to her baby," he mused. "She's trying to protect Grace from all the bad things in life."

He wondered how Susanna could do that. She had clearly come up against some pretty mean times. It was obvious from the fact that she arrived in town on the run with a broken-down car and no money. The little she'd said about her ex-husband had been just as telling. And yet, somehow, she found the way to sing an uplifting song to her child, to pretend that things were better than they were.

He wasn't sure he could do that. He'd probably never tried. The thought that Susanna was making such an effort amazed him, humbled him, and he was drawn from his chair to the door, out into the hallway, to the back of the house.

He walked silently, he listened.

And then she was there, with her hair tousled as if she'd been snuggling Grace and her face pink and aglow from the heat of the dryer.

She was folding clothes. Brady looked down at her hands and saw that she was smoothing her fingertips over a pair of his black boxers.

His breath froze, his brain all but stopped functioning, his body grew instantly hard. If he could have retreated, he would have, but instead he stood there, feeling the sweat form on his brow, trying to force away the ache and desire that coursed through his body.

Susanna looked up then, straight into his eyes, and her fingers stopped moving. The pale skin of her neck turned a lovely pink. She opened her lips to speak, her eyes wide and frantic and embarrassed.

And Brady could no more have stopped himself from moving to her than he could have stopped the moon from rising. He reached out as if to take the cloth from beneath her fingertips, but instead his own fingers raked the bare skin of her arm. He slid his hand upward, over her elbow, cupping her shoulder, lightly brushing her collarbone and then cupping her jaw.

"I'll take this," he said, meaning to take what she was holding, but instead he leaned in and took her lips beneath his own. He brushed her mouth with his, he teased her upper lip with his tongue, and then he brushed her mouth again.

She was soft, the softest, sweetest thing he'd ever tasted.

Her warm breath joined with his. Shaky, uneven. Her hands rose to rest on his chest. His heart pounded beneath her palms.

"Brady?" she asked softly when he pulled back for a second. And the uncertainty in her voice, the sure knowledge that she had been misused by a man before and didn't deserve to have it happen again, stopped him cold.

He stared at her for a second, then whisked his boxers from where they had fallen on the top of the dryer. "This was a bad idea," he said.

And he walked away as swiftly as his bad leg would allow him to. He turned once before leaving the room. She was standing there silent, her face as pale as paper, her eyes as wounded as eyes could get.

"I'm sorry," he managed to say. "And thank you for washing my clothes. I do appreciate it." But of course nothing he could say would make any difference. As always, it was what he'd done rather than what he'd said that made the difference. And as he'd learned in the past, some things just couldn't be undone.

He had overstepped the boundaries. He had hurt her, and now she was going to run.

No doubt that was a good thing.

Susanna sat in bed that night, her fingers pressed to her lips. The memory of Brady kissing her wouldn't leave her alone.

He had been gentle, so very gentle at first, his touch achingly wonderful, luring her, seducing her until she had almost forgotten who she was and what she was and all the things she had promised herself she would never forget.

Men were risky things, dangerous things. A woman who had had her experiences could not afford romantic notions. Or passion.

And yet…there was Brady gazing at her with that heated look in his deep blue eyes, Brady touching her, stroking her, Brady melting her resolve.

Grace shifted in her sleep and Susanna looked to where her daughter lay.

"Don't worry, little one," she promised. "Mommy would never let us get back into the place where we were. No man is going to make us forget that we have to stand alone."

But darn it, Brady Malone had sure come close today.

Susanna would have smiled at the thought if it hadn't been so frightening. She turned out the light, slid deeper into the bed and pulled the covers up, staring out at the moon that shone through the curtainless windows.

For long minutes she lay there, listening to the night sounds and her heartbeat. In time, she heard the soft sound of a door opening and a low woof. Brady was letting Scrap out.

The urge to rise from her bed and go to Brady was almost overwhelming, and because she felt such a strong desire she fought it. She didn't want to feel this kind of yearning for a man's touch, his presence, his scent.

But she did. What was she going to do about that?

"Forget about it," she whispered. "Keep doing what you're doing. Go on as you have been."

Eventually she would have to leave anyway. Sooner or later, she would start to worry about what was going on with Trent. Her ex-husband was a jealously possessive man. Maybe he was still looking for her and maybe if he dug deep enough he would find her.

She would give anything to prevent Trent from finding her and Grace. And that meant that she and Brady would be parting pretty soon. Susanna ached at the thought. Already she was feeling at home at Red Rose. She and Grace were becoming a part of things. Even this building that Brady was lending her had taken on the feel of home.

And the man across the way?

Susanna tried not to think of him, but still the thoughts came unbidden. She wondered if she would kiss Brady one more time before she had to go.

Chapter Six

What was the woman doing now? Brady wondered the next evening. The clink of metal against metal drifted to him. He heard what sounded like a muffled curse, which just didn't seem right. Susanna wasn't the kind to curse.

He glanced at Scrap who had his long ears pricked up. Scrap looked a little eager.

"All right, all right, we'll go check it out," Brady promised.

Immediately, Scrap jumped up and trotted to the door. For a middle-aged dog, he certainly perked up at the thought of going to see Susanna and Grace.

"Goofy dog," Brady said, but he had to admit that his own step was a bit lighter today. He should never have kissed her. He cursed himself for having done so, but at least now he knew how she tasted. Like a feast that a man wanted to take part in again and again.

He nearly tripped over Scrap.

"Darn it, dog, at least wait until I get the door open." And he pulled back the door, freeing his great lion of a pet to go galloping across the grass.

He followed more slowly, studying Susanna as he moved.

"What exactly are you doing?" he asked.

"Yikes!" She shrieked and dropped the screwdriver she was holding. When she bent and picked it up, her blond hair fell forward like fluid silk. It caught on her cheek when she rose, her face flushed and pretty. "What am I doing? Well..." She held out a brassy-looking contraption, a screwdriver and hammer. "I thought I was putting on a dead bolt. I got this book from the library that explains how to do it and made it look pretty easy, but—" a frown furrowed her brow "—I don't quite seem to have gotten the hang of it yet."

"A dead bolt?" He felt the anger rising to a boil inside of him, and she wasn't the one he was mad at.

"For the door," she explained.

"I know what a dead bolt is for. You think one is necessary?"

She shifted a bit from one foot to the other like a guilty child. "Yes, well, I know I should have asked you if you minded me messing with your doors, but...it is improving the property. I didn't think you would care all that much. I'm sorry to have presumed."

"You're apologizing to me?"

"Yes, I—"

"Susanna, I'll be damned if I tell you again that I'm sorry I kissed you, even if I know darn well I should never have touched you. But as Scrap is my witness, I would never force you, never touch you if you asked me not to.''

She blinked those beautiful green eyes.

"You think I'm doing this because I'm afraid you're going to pounce on me?"

"Again? You're afraid I'm going to pounce on you again."

"I most certainly am not. And I wouldn't call what you did pouncing anyway."

She looked completely indignant, her slender arms crossed, her chin jutting out, fire flashing in those lovely eyes. Brady had the feeling that he had completely offended her.

"What would you call it then? What I did?"

Susanna stared directly into his eyes, then quickly looked away. Her fingers reached as if to touch her lips, as if remembering the kiss, before she quickly lowered her hand. "I would call it coaxing," she said, "or caressing. Maybe stroking or even just kissing, but I did not feel pounced on, and I wasn't afraid of you."

He closed his eyes for a brief second and released a long breath. Thank goodness. When he'd seen her so determined to seal that door...

"But you're afraid of something?" he asked, motioning to the dead bolt.

She looked to the side, then back at him. "I would just feel more comfortable if I had an extra lock."

He couldn't help it then. "Did he hit you?"

She shook her head. "My ex-husband, Trent? No, but he said things, lots of things, and when I tried to leave him, he kept trying to stop me. He kept showing up, even after the divorce was over. I would come home and he would be there, even if I changed the locks. I learned to hang the towels in a certain way, stack the dishes in a certain way, leave something just inside the door so that it had to be moved to walk across the room. If I came back and any of those things had changed, I knew he was there or had been there, and I ran. He wouldn't have hurt me, but it was...creepy.''

''There are laws against such things.''

''I never had any proof. He would leave if I called the police, but he would come right back. He would lie and say that I was crazy, that he had never been in the house. He always made sure there was no hard evidence that he had been. But all that's behind me now,'' she said with the worst example of mock cheerfulness Brady had ever witnessed.

He wanted to ask if she was sure her ex-husband was gone for good, but obviously she wasn't sure if she was dead-bolting her doors. And also obviously, she was still afraid of the man.

''Your ex-husband was at fault, Susanna. You're not blaming yourself, are you?''

''No, I'm not, but I'm not going to be stupid and fail to take precautions, either. Not that I think he'd get close. You and Scrap are right next door, after all.''

Brady almost smiled. ''You think we make good watchdogs?''

''You look intimidating.''

That gave him pause. ''I wouldn't purposely hurt you, Susanna, but don't start thinking that I'm a white knight.''

She shook her head. ''I don't expect anything of you, Brady.''

''That's not what I meant.''

"Why do you paint yourself as such a bad guy, some black knight?"

"Surely you've heard stories."

"I heard that your father wasn't very nice and that your brother wasn't, either. No one gave me any specifics. They respected your privacy, for the most part."

"Well then, they didn't tell you that I got in trouble for stealing a car when I was fifteen, or that I got caught drinking underage several times, or that I thought every Friday at school was set aside for fighting. I broke into a house when I was nineteen. The judge sentenced me to either jail or the army."

She nodded. "I heard the part about the army."

"It changed me, but not enough. I let my friend get in a car when he was drunk. I walked away with a bum knee. He didn't walk away at all. Nothing can change that, and nothing can erase the things I've done."

"But you're not doing them now."

"That doesn't make much difference. Essentially I'm still the same man. I like my life, but I don't feel comfortable with what you're trying to make me into. I don't want to be that man."

"You'd rather think you're bad."

He stared at her for a long time. "I didn't tell you all the things I'd done. Let's just leave it at that." He took the dead bolt and tools from her hand, squatted and started to work on the door.

Susanna came up and stood behind his back. He could feel her heat, smell the clean, soap smell of her.

"Did you ever try to kill anyone?" she asked.

"No. But I would have if I'd had to. It's what soldiers do."

"That's not what I meant, and you know it."

"Then, no, I never tried to kill anyone, but I sometimes wished that certain people would disappear off the face of the earth and make my life easier."

"Everyone gets like that sometimes. Did you ever hit a woman or a child?"

"I never did that," he admitted, "and I don't intend to start now."

"Well, then, did you—"

"Susanna?" His voice dropped to a hoarse whisper.

"Yes?"

"Stop. Please. Leave it."

"All right. Thank you, Brady, for fixing my door."

Her door. She said it so proudly, as if she'd never had a door. Maybe she hadn't. Maybe that jerk she'd married had made her feel as if she owed him everything.

When Susanna left to go check on Grace, Brady looked down at Scrap. "This lock is an improvement, buddy, but I'll bet we could do better than this. Maybe some paint, maybe some furniture. A woman should have her own things."

Scrap gazed at him with doggie love in his eyes.

"Don't you start, Scrap. I am nobody's white knight. There's too much black in my heart and too much past in my life, and nothing's going to change that."

Nothing was going to change the fact that he couldn't kiss Susanna again, either. But he wanted to.

Oh, yes, he wanted to kiss her and to take her into his bed and show her gentleness and passion something awful.

Even black knights had dreams, he guessed.

* * *

When Susanna came home from work the next day, not only did her house have a dead bolt and chain-lock system, but half of it was painted a gorgeous sea green. Brady was on the far side, shirtless, wearing a pair of white painter's pants and a white baseball cap turned backward.

"What's this?" she asked.

He paused in midstroke.

"Paint."

"I can see that. The question is why?"

"It needed it."

She looked at his house that was also in need of a coat of paint. Amazing. He had the latest and greatest technology inside his house, but little in the way of decor, and the outside of his house had only been maintained in the most rudimentary fashion. It was a place to live, but not really a home.

"You could use that on your house someday," she said.

He paused and stared at her. "I might someday." Somehow she knew that he wouldn't. Any color that was added to his house wouldn't be coming from his own paintbrush, and she didn't think she was capable of tackling a paint job the size of Brady's house. But maybe she could do something else.

A sudden idea made her smile. Brady Malone might think of himself as a bad guy, but she knew quite a bit about bad guys and black knights. He didn't really qualify, at least not where she was concerned.

And she intended to show him that. She knew just how.

* * *

So, her ex-husband hadn't known how to exit gracefully, had he? Brady continued to ponder that tidbit of information that evening as he and Scrap ate their dinner. Scrap, as usual, had no table manners and sloshed water all over the plastic place mat Brady had placed beneath his dish.

"The man was harassing her, boy, trying to scare her or to force her to take him back. Sounds like he was a possessive bully. No wonder she ran." And she had run right to him, Brady knew, not because she'd wanted to but because she'd had no choice. That meant the rules he played by had to be stricter than ever. He couldn't take advantage of her situation. He couldn't touch her the way he wanted to, especially when he had nothing lasting to offer her. All he could do was give her a place to stay while she needed and wanted it. And he could do one thing more.

"If he ever shows up here, he'll wish that he hadn't." Of course, he couldn't stop the man from coming. He had no hard and fast idea of where the guy was right now. Neither did Susanna, and Brady knew that was what was scaring her. He hated the thought that she had any reason to be scared. He wanted to reassure her that he would protect her. To do that, he needed more information, information she couldn't give him.

But if there was anything he knew about, it was how to get information. Not that there had been that much information on the Net about Susanna when he had looked her up the other day. An address in Chicago, not much else, which was a very good thing. She had obviously lived a very quiet life, and now that would work to her advantage. He hoped that her ex-husband was a different story.

What had she said his name was? Trent? How about the last name? Same as hers?

Brady took a gamble and tried that. He turned to his computer and typed the name Trent Wright into the search engine. He found out quite a few things, a few lawsuits that had been filed either by him or against him, some information on his gambling habits, which Brady had to use some unethical procedures to find, some news clippings linking Trent Wright to several sleazy women. The guy didn't seem to worry too much about bad publicity. Unfortunately the chief bit of information, where the man was now, just wasn't there. Or if it was there, it was buried too deep to locate in a short period of time.

And ten minutes later, the whole picture changed. Brady swore softly to himself. Something was there online that shouldn't have been and that hadn't been there earlier. Not pertaining to Trent Wright but to Susanna Wright. An announcement on the Red Rose Web site about the fact that there were newcomers in town.

Brady turned to Scrap. "Dammit boy, this thing has been online for a couple of days. I wonder how many people have seen it. I wonder if our boy Trent has seen it. This could lead him straight to her."

He ran his hands through his hair. "I am not a white knight," he said, looking down at his dog.

And if Trent Wright took one step toward Susanna, every dark force that lived within his soul would come bubbling to the surface, Brady reasoned.

Just let the man even try to intimidate or to scare her again. Just let him think about stalking her.

"So how do we keep an eye on her without giving her and everyone else the wrong impression, boy?" he asked his pet.

Scrap looked at his master with big, trusting eyes and gave out one deep-throated woof. It wasn't really an answer, but it mirrored the consternation Brady was feeling.

There wasn't any good way to go about this, but there wasn't any choice, either. He couldn't ignore the gut feeling he had that Susanna needed a protector, but he had no legal basis to demand protection of the local sheriff, either.

"Looks like our life is about to change, Scrap," he said.

But then it already had. For the past few days his whole world had been different. He thought of Susanna's lips beneath his own and almost groaned. She had awakened things inside him that he didn't want to examine.

But like it or not, she was his to protect now, and he intended to do that, in whatever way he could.

When Susanna finally got a chance to take a break the next day, she placed Grace in her umbrella stroller, rolled her out onto the sidewalk in front of the Red Rose Café and very nearly ran over Brady, who was parked right outside the café.

She took a deep breath. "What on earth are you doing here?"

His abashed smile took her breath away. "Cluttering the sidewalk?"

She rolled her eyes. "You do that a lot?"

"Not really. I'm not a town person usually."

"But today?"

He shoved his hands into his pockets and rocked back on his heels. It was an "aw, shucks" look that didn't fit a man who usually radiated confidence and presence. "Today I'm looking to rent some office space. I thought that building right across the street might do. I was just viewing it from this angle."

She cocked her head, confused. "Why are you renting office space? And what does it matter what it looks like from this angle?"

"Expanding the business," he said brusquely. "And since so many people come into Red Rose by way of the café, I wanted to see if a sign on the second floor of my new building would catch their attention when they walked outside."

He sounded uncertain, and so Susanna couldn't help but reach out and touch his arm, even though the feel of his skin beneath her fingertips reminded her that he was not usually a man who radiated uncertainty. Usually he radiated confidence, strength, virility...

She snatched her hand back. "It's an excellent idea. What exactly is your business, anyway?"

"I invent computer software to help people run their businesses."

"Well, then, opening an office in Red Rose is probably an excellent idea. I'll be sure and mention you to any of my customers."

"You don't have to do that," he said quickly.

"But I want to."

"I wish you wouldn't."

"There aren't any strings attached."

Suddenly the strong, confident man was back. Brady's eyes were fierce. "You think I don't know that?"

"I wouldn't blame you if you didn't know that. After all, I come to town, a woman alone, and I've relied on you to help me time and time again. You must be wishing you could get me out of your hair."

He stared into her eyes. He reached out suddenly and took her chin in his hand. "You really think that?"

"You like to be alone."

"I do."

"Well, then... I keep making your life messy and complicating things. Just so you know, I'm not going to keep doing that forever. I'm looking for a new place."

He opened his mouth, then closed it again. "I hope you find a nice one, but just so *you* know, I don't let people complicate my life. If I'm doing something, it's my choice, not my obligation."

At that moment Grace let out a small squeal of dismay. Susanna leaned over her daughter, but Brady had already dropped to one knee.

"What's the matter, Gracie girl?" he asked.

Gracie moaned and reached down. The rubber dog she liked to chew on had fallen to the ground. Brady snatched it up, and Grace raised both arms pleadingly, her blue eyes laden with unshed tears.

"You're breaking my heart," he said gently, brushing one index finger across her baby cheek, "but I have to go wash this first before I give it back to you." And without another word, he disappeared into the café. Susanna heard the group sigh when he walked in, just before the door closed behind him.

"Okay, we owe him one more," Susanna whispered fiercely to her daughter, kissing Grace on the forehead. "Just don't fall in love with him, sweetie.

He's being so nice to us, but he's too much of a gentleman to admit that we're taking advantage of the situation. He wants to be alone. We have to get out soon and leave him alone. And in the meantime," she said, eyeing the empty windows of the second floor across the way, "we will too send customers his way. He came to town to get them, and we pour their coffee every day. Helping Brady enlarge his business is one thing we can do to show our gratitude."

Because she certainly couldn't show it the way her body and heart were telling her to, by wrapping her arms and lips around his tall, strong frame.

"First thing tomorrow, we start our campaign to show the town that Brady isn't the kind of man he thinks he is." Somehow she had to let him know that he really wasn't a black knight. He was, instead, the most honest, caring man she'd ever met.

Chapter Seven

Had he really stood there and lied to her? Brady asked himself after he'd said goodbye to Susanna and she had gone on her way. After she'd been married to a first-class creep who'd probably lied to her many times?

"That's exactly what I did," Brady muttered to himself, cursing his ornery hide.

"Brady?"

Brady noticed Sunny Delavan standing in front of him on the sidewalk. She gave him a long look, placing her hands on her ample hips and studying him hard. "Under normal circumstances I haven't seen you anywhere outside the Piggly Wiggly over in Lindley Junction in years," she said. "Did you lose something? Did Susanna's car break down again?"

He returned Sunny's assessing look. "Her car is fine. I just had some business to take care of."

She raised one brow. "Susanna business?"

He frowned. "Business."

Suddenly the big woman smiled. "She's a sweetie, isn't she? Just makes you want to wrap her up in something warm and take care of her and that little baby."

He looked to the side. "I'm sure Susanna is a very nice woman."

Sunny nodded. "She certainly is. I would be very upset if any man took her for a ride or caused her grief. She's already had enough of that."

Brady's disposition lifted. He leveled a look at Sunny. "Then you and I are in agreement, Sunny. She's had more than enough of that. I wouldn't want to hear that anyone was giving her trouble or making her sad."

"And if you did?"

"I've been known to break a few things, if you remember."

Sunny laughed. Brady had once gotten into a fight in the middle of her dairy shop. "Still hot-tempered?"

He slowly shook his head. "Hot tempers are for the young, but sometimes even a grown man needs to be reminded that women are not to be mistreated."

"I always did like something about you, Brady."

"Probably my habit of downing huge chocolate malts when I was young."

"Probably," she said with a chuckle. "Will you be doing lots of business in town in the future?"

There it was, that lie he'd woven again. But there wasn't any way he was going to come right out and admit the truth, that he had come to town because he was worried that Susanna's ex-husband might show up and do something terrible one day. He might well be wrong, and even if he wasn't, there was no way he was going to scare Susanna by even hinting at the possibility.

"You might see me in town now and then," he admitted. And he nodded to Sunny and moved on.

"Abby, do you have any roses?" Susanna asked after work that day. "I mean, roses that look like they need more love and attention than usual? I don't have all that much money to spend. Oh, and petunias. Pink and white and purple ones, I think, if you have them."

"Ones that need an extra dollop of nurturing?" Abby teased.

"Yes, like the Christmas tree that Charlie Brown bought."

Abby smiled and nodded. "I have just the thing. My forgotten babies that got caught out in that wind that came through the other day. Now they're orphan flowers that no one wants. I'll be glad to find someone to give them a home." She led Susanna and Grace to the back of the nursery where a pitiful group of plants were waiting. Just what Susanna wanted.

"How much?" she asked.

Abby named a ridiculously low price.

"Are you offering me charity?" Susanna asked.

"I'm parting with my babies in the hopes that you'll breathe new life into them," Abby countered. "Believe me, no one else wants them."

"You could salvage them."

"Yes, but I'm planning a wedding. You're practically panting for the opportunity. I'm grateful. You must have a special place for them."

She did. A very special place. She wasn't sure these plants would be welcome there, but she had to try.

And as she measured out her money into Abby's hand, Susanna had to try one more thing. "Thank you, Abby. I'll do my best to make them big and strong."

"What more could a plant nut like me ask? Anything else?"

"Just one more thing. Brady Malone is opening an office up in town."

"You're kidding."

"No, he's thinking of expanding his business. You know he invents software for small businesses?"

"I think I might have. I never really paid much attention to what Brady did, although I'd heard plenty of negative things. He never seemed to like people poking into his life, and I have to respect that."

"Well, he's coming back into town now, so if you ever need something new...would you keep him in mind?"

Abby looked at Susanna as if she had grown pointed ears. "Brady is asking you to advertise for him?"

"He wouldn't do that. You know that, don't you?"

Abby shrugged. "I'd like to think that, but the truth is that I don't know much about Brady at all. He hasn't been around much these past few years and when he was younger, well..."

"He was a kid."

"I know."

"Was he so bad?"

Abby wrinkled her brow. "You know, I don't really know. I never really knew him. Not personally. But his father and his brother were scary, and there were stories..."

"Which you believe."

Abby shook her head again. "I'm not sure I do…or if I don't, for that matter. I certainly wouldn't want to condemn an innocent man. It's just…"

"What?"

"It's just that I know what it is to be hurt by a man, Susanna. Before I met Griffin, I allowed myself to be hurt that way. I think you've been hurt, too. I wouldn't want to see it happen again. Just make sure that you know all the facts before you end up getting hurt again."

Susanna looked into Abby's gentle eyes. She knew that the woman was right. She didn't know any more about Brady than anyone else did. In fact, she knew less. But darn it, he had been nice to her. She felt safe with him nearby, and it had been so long since she had felt truly safe.

"I'll do that," she said weakly. She didn't want to be careful where Brady was concerned. She wanted to rush headlong into madness, right where he didn't want to go and where neither of them should be thinking of going. But there was Grace to think of. She only had one mother to care for her and to protect her and love her.

"I promise you that I'm not going to do anything risky when I have a child to look after," she said softly. And suddenly the pretty pink and purple petunias looked sadder, but she knew that Abby was right.

Abby nodded and ran a hand over her own growing abdomen. She had been pregnant when she'd met Griffin O'Dell. Susanna had heard that. Abby was right to urge caution. She knew all about risky relationships. The fact that she had finally found her one good man didn't negate the past or the lessons learned from it. "Come on, I'll help you get those out to the car."

Susanna smiled, but crossed her arms. "Absolutely not. You shouldn't be lugging heavy flats of flowers around. Do me a favor and keep an eye on Grace while I get these outside. I'm temporarily a little bit down on my luck financially, but I'm far from helpless."

Abby laughed. She smiled down at Grace and made way for Susanna to take the plants. "Go for it, then. Grace and I will tell each other gardening secrets while you demonstrate your strength and independence."

Susanna wrinkled her nose and chuckled as she picked up the first flat of flowers. But the reality was that Abby wasn't that far from the truth. Susanna had a real need to show herself and the world that she could take care of her child and herself and a few other things, as well. She could be strong and stand on her own feet. That was why she had to pay back Brady every time he helped her, she reminded herself. It had nothing at all to do with the way her heart grew wings whenever he stared at her with those fierce blue eyes. She just wanted to be his equal, his friend, nothing more, and that was why she was here.

Several hours later, after sneaking into her house with a bucket of forest-green paint and a brush, she gazed at her handiwork.

"Not bad, Grace, do you think?"

Grace looked at the plain wooden boxes that her mother had painted. "Buh?" she said.

"That's right, sweetie, they're for Brady. I'm going to plant petunias in the boxes and plant roses next to his steps. Not sure when. He always seems to be around. Maybe in the dark of night. I want this to be a surprise."

And that's just what she did. Creeping out hours later, Susanna quietly lugged the boxes over to Brady's house. Scrap gave a slight whine, but she whispered love words to him and he calmed right down. Holding a flashlight in one hand and using an old hand spade from the garage, Susanna quietly dug two holes and gently slipped the roses in, patting the dirt down. She would have liked to mix in some peat moss, but this was the best she could manage for now. Taking the dirt she had removed for the roses, plus a little more, she almost filled the boxes, nestled the petunias in their new homes and then quickly gave them a final layer of soil. She moved back to look, shining her flashlight on each box and then smiled to herself as she turned to walk back to her own side of the property.

"Don't take another step. I don't care much for trespassers." The deep voice came from the shadows of the porch.

Susanna started to whirl around just as Brady's arms caught her from behind. She nearly lost the baby monitor she had clipped to her waistband. She did drop the flashlight and spade and they hit the ground with a thud somewhere near her feet. She gasped. "I—I didn't think of it as trespassing." Her voice came out weak and frightened.

"Dammit! Dammit, Susanna, what in hell were you doing? I thought you were...hell, I don't know... I thought you were a stranger. I might have hurt you. Did I hurt you? What were you doing wandering around in the middle of the night? I didn't hurt you, did I?"

He dragged her closer against him, nestling her in the vee between his spread legs as he gently ran one hand up and down her arm, up the side of her neck, his fingers caressing her jaw.

"Are you all right?" he asked.

She managed to nod against his fingertips in spite of the fact that in the dark, with his hands sliding over her body, she was all too aware of every nerve ending her skin possessed. "I'm...I'm fine," she whispered. "You can let me go now."

He did. Very slowly he released her and turned her in his arms to face him. The darkness hid his features and without her flashlight she couldn't make out his expression, but she knew what his eyes would look like, anyway. He was angry.

She shivered slightly.

"Dammit," he groaned. "I hurt you, didn't I?"

Quickly she shook her head. "No, really, I'm fine, and I don't blame you for being angry. I should have told you I was coming. I just wanted everything to be a surprise."

He cupped her jaw again. "Everything?"

His fingertip touched the pulse in her neck, and her whole body came to life. "Yes, the flowers."

"Flowers." He raked his knuckles across her cheek. She wished she had put on a bra beneath her T-shirt because her breasts were revealing exactly what his touch was doing to her, and this close to him, she had a feeling he would soon know.

"Roses. And petunias," she offered weakly. "I planted them for you. They're a little scrawny right now, but they'll be pretty soon."

"You planted flowers for me?" His voice came out low and rough and uncertain. "Why?"

"You wouldn't take my money. You painted my house and brought me things. You protected us and took us off the street. Did you think I would just let that pass?"

"I didn't ask for payment."

"I know, and that made me want to pay you even more. You gave to me without asking for anything in return. I wanted to give you something. I needed to give you something wonderful."

"Something wonderful," he said, and his voice was practically a caress. Suddenly the dark seemed warmer, the night turned golden in spite of the fact that there was no moon.

"Something magical," she agreed, and she rose up on her toes. His arms slipped beneath hers, his big hands splaying across her back, then slipping beneath her shirt to slide up her bare skin. Lifting her slightly, bending nearer, he brought his lips almost to hers, but not quite close enough.

She was pressed against him, her breasts molded to his bare chest, his arms strong around her, and Susanna knew she was about to do what she had told Abby she wouldn't do. She was going to leap from careful to crazy. With one quiet, swift move, she reached up and twined her arms around Brady's neck, pulling him close, and then she opened her mouth beneath his. She nibbled at his lower lip, sucking in the fullness.

He groaned and pulled back slightly. "You make me crazy," he whispered. "You've made me insane to touch you since the moment I saw you. I shouldn't even be thinking of you, but..."

And then he uttered a soft curse and crushed her to him. He fed on her, he brushed her lips with his, making her want more, and still more. His hands searched her skin, sliding down to the indentation at her waist, resting there for a moment, then climbing to brush just the underside of her breasts.

She jerked and pressed harder against him.

"Flowers," he said with disbelief. "The woman comes out at midnight to plant flowers for me. What kind of woman does that?"

"A grateful one," she whispered and kissed him.

"A careless one," he said against her lips. "A woman a man should not take advantage of just because he found her outside his house in the dark."

And like that, Susanna realized what she was doing. She was pushing herself on Brady. What's more, she was taking advantage of the night and the ease with which forbidden things were done in the darkness. Even though, when the morning came, nothing would have changed.

Slowly she eased away from him. "You're right that we shouldn't be doing this, Brady," she said, gazing up toward him, "but I don't think you were the one taking advantage of the situation. You are a man who knows how to kiss a woman." She instilled her voice with as much confidence as she could muster. There wasn't any way she was going to let him think of her as the fragile female and himself as the predator male. She knew what a predator male was like, and he wasn't it. The fact that he didn't want a woman in his life wasn't something he should be made to feel guilty for. And so, not bothering to look for her spade or her flashlight, she walked away with as much swagger as she could muster.

"Enjoy the flowers, Brady. They're going to add something nice to your life."

"Susanna?"

She stopped, afraid to turn around for fear she would go running back across the yard. "What?"

The silence stretched out for several seconds. "You won't come around this late anymore, will you? I'm only a man."

She forced steel into her spine. "I won't do it again," she promised. But as for the part about Brady being only a man, he was so very wrong. She was terribly afraid that he was becoming the man she wanted too much.

Chapter Eight

An unknown man had recently been a visitor to the Red Rose message board on the Web site, Brady noted. Sure, the guy had used the screen name Justice, not Trent Wright, but he had asked questions about newcomers, women in particular, especially women with babies. He claimed that he wanted a ready-made family, and Lorelei Jasons, who ran the Web site, told him that if he was looking for a wife, he couldn't do better than Red Rose.

Of course, Brady thought, drinking his third morning cup of coffee, there was no real proof that the message was from a man looking for his ex-wife, but he had a strong suspicion that it was.

Red Rose had been a town in need of men for a long time. The townspeople hadn't made any secret of it. Any man seriously bent on finding a wife here would know that and simply come to see what he could see. Unless, of course, the man was looking for one particular woman and wasn't quite sure where she

was. Unless the man had read the News Notes section
that the Web site had posted three days earlier, where
Lorelei had mentioned that there were two new faces
in town. She hadn't named names. Lorelei was careful
about such things, but even that much had been too
much, and as soon as Brady had seen it, he had done
what he had never done before. He had sent a message to Lorelei, explaining Susanna's situation and
asking her to be even more careful from here on out.
Hence, Lorelei's vague answer to the man's question.

"I should have been on top of that Web site
sooner," Brady muttered, leaning back so that the
front legs of his chair were off the ground. But he
hadn't been, and now who knew if Trent Wright was
on Susanna's trail or not?

"I have to go to town, Scrap," Brady said, letting
the chair down with a clatter of wood on wood.
"Sorry you have to stay here, but they don't allow
dogs in the café."

And they didn't allow men to kiss the waitresses,
either, Brady reminded himself, thinking of the way
Susanna had fit against him last night. She had felt
so right, even though touching her had been wrong.

She had planted flowers for him! This morning
he'd awakened to look out and see their fragile and
bruised but colorful petals waving at him in the
breeze.

What kind of man would let a woman like that get
away?

A man who didn't deserve her, Brady thought. *He*
didn't deserve her. Neither did Trent Wright, but he
was pretty sure the man would put two and two together and show up here sooner or later. It might take
a while. Brady had added Susanna's name to several

other towns' guestbooks in an attempt to lead the man astray. He hoped it worked.

But if it didn't, well...

"I really need another cup of coffee," he told his dog, and he knew right where to find the best cup and the prettiest, sweetest waitress a man could ever know.

Susanna circled the room doling out coffee and scrambled eggs and smiles. "Good morning," she said to a serious dark-haired man sitting at a table in the back corner. "May I help you? Coffee? Breakfast?"

"Good morning," he said politely but without a smile. "Yes to coffee, but decaf please. No to breakfast. I'm afraid I'm in a bit of a hurry."

"Then I'll hurry, too," she said. "The decaf is in another pot. I'll be right back."

"I'm sorry to be rushing you."

"Don't worry about it. I'm here to help the customers."

"Hey, Lon, got a big case today?" Lydia called.

He almost smiled, Susanna thought as she came back with the decaf. "Every case is big, Lydia," he said, and he concentrated on putting cream and sugar in his coffee.

Just then the door opened and Brady stepped in. As always, he seemed to fill the room with his presence. Susanna had to hold herself back from rushing over to him, especially when he looked straight at her. By the intensity of his gaze, she could almost imagine that he was remembering her limp body coiled against his strong, hard one last night. But she was probably wrong. Like the man she'd just served, Brady was probably just thinking about getting to his business fast.

"I'll be right there," she said, hoping her voice didn't betray her thoughts, doing her best to look calm and unflustered.

"No hurry," he said in that way he had that made her think that he would never be in a hurry, especially not when he was making love to a woman.

She nearly dropped the coffeepot right there on the floor.

But then she noticed that Brady had stiffened. His look had turned cautious. He was staring past her shoulder.

She turned to look behind her and saw the man she'd just served staring back at Brady with open hatred in his eyes. He had seemed like such a nice man, a kind man. What on earth?

Susanna glanced back at Brady, but a mask had come over him. The man behind her moved up beside her and thrust money in her hand. "I'm sure that will more than cover things," he said quietly, and then before she could even register how much money he had given her, he nodded to Lydia and left the café.

Brady's jaw was like a steel blade. She was sure he was going to leave, too, but then he looked at her. She had never seen a man who seemed more alone. She had no idea what this was all about. Most likely she should just go on about her business, go back to the kitchen and compose herself, ask some questions of Lydia or Sunny or someone else who could fill her in before she did or said something reckless.

Instead her legs carried her across the room. She gazed up at Brady. "Are you staying?" she asked softly.

He stared down at her. She had the distinct feeling that he would like nothing better than to walk out that door and never look back.

She waited. She tried not to want him to stay. She made a real effort to control her reaction to the man, knowing what a mistake it would be to grow to care for a man like Brady Malone.

His eyes were hard, his body was hard; he left no room for softness in his life; he didn't want anything to do with the town or any woman.

But as she stood there waiting, he stared directly into her eyes, he glanced down at her hand that still held the coffeepot. She realized that she was trembling slightly.

"I'm staying," he said, as if he had made some difficult decision. "I've got business in town."

Ah, yes, she'd almost forgotten. He hadn't come here to see her, but to see about opening that office.

Which was the way it should be, Susanna thought as Brady took a seat and she poured him a cup of coffee. The room had grown silent during the wordless exchange between the man in the corner and Brady. Now the chatter seemed to pick up and swell, growing artificially loud. The women at the nearby tables kept glancing at Brady who had pulled out some paperwork and was studying it, but looked up every time the bell over the door signaled a newcomer. What was going on here?

Susanna didn't know, but she intended to find out. She wandered over to Lydia.

"I have to go see to Grace for a moment," she said. Nothing unusual about that. She did it all the time, and Lydia was most understanding about the demands of motherhood, but this time Susanna frowned at her and glanced over her shoulder at Brady.

Lydia nodded. She followed Susanna to the back of the dining area where Grace was seated on a customer's lap, babbling alternately to a squeaky toy she was clutching and to the woman who held her. The padded penned-off play area Lydia had provided had hardly been used. Everyone seemed to want to hold Grace.

"You're going to be spoiled silly, sweetie," Susanna said, but she smiled at the woman and lifted Grace into her arms. "Thank you," she told her temporary voluntary baby-sitter.

"She's a little love," the woman answered, and Susannah's heart swelled. In so many ways Red Rose seemed the perfect place to settle. If only she hadn't met Brady, and if only she wasn't attracted to him. Because he made staying here impossible. Getting too close to him, and she was doing that, she realized, was going to prove disastrous. In more ways than one, she was sure. She just wasn't sure what all the ways were. There was so much she didn't know about him.

She carried Grace into the kitchen with Lydia on her heels.

"What was that exchange between Brady and that man?" Susanna said as soon as she cleared the door. "And why is everyone acting so strange around Brady?"

Lydia shrugged. "If you mean Lon Banks, well, I don't know all that's between Lon and Brady, although I know they have a history. Brady's brother was the hit-and-run driver that cost Lon the full use of his right arm. He'd been a promising baseball player before that. As for the women, well…you know that Brady doesn't come into town. Even if he weren't such a ruggedly handsome man, there would be talk if he suddenly showed up. He's more than a bit notorious, and with that military manner, he can give people the shivers. And given his obvious masculinity in a café that tends to be most frequented by females, well, add that to the dangerous part and…''

She didn't have to say more. The women of Red Rose were fluttering and flustered because Brady was a good-looking man with a bad reputation.

"Wonder why he's here, anyway," Lydia said, giving Susanna a speculative look. "He's managed to stay away all of his adult life, yet now, only days after I hire a charming and pretty waitress…''

If Susanna had thought what Lydia was hinting at had even a fragment of truth to it, she might have been blushing, but she knew darn well Brady's being here had nothing to do with her. He'd made it clear that while he desired her, he wasn't at all happy about it. If he had his way, he'd never see her at all.

"I think I might have mentioned that he's opening an office in town. I don't think he likes the thought, but…well, you know how business is, especially the computer business. Expand or grow stagnant. He's here because his business is going to be here.''

Lydia raised one brow.

Susanna raised a brow herself, offering a challenge. "He's not here for me, and I have to tell you that I'm betting he's really uncomfortable. His past, whatever it may be, dogs him. Everyone thinks he's bad. He thinks he's bad. All that whispering is bound to emphasize that and bring up unwelcome memories of the past.''

Lydia crossed her arms although her expression

was kind. "I like you, Susanna. I like you a lot, but are you suggesting that I try to control my customers?"

Susanna let out a sigh. "No, I guess I'm not. I just wish there was something I could do. That man left because Brady was here. I suspect that everyone but me knew that, and Brady knows that they know."

Lydia patted Susanna's hand. "It's just human nature, Susanna. Some things you can't change."

Susanna supposed Lydia was right, but she wished she were wrong. Surely there was something a person could do.

After Lydia left, Susanna hugged her daughter tight and gave her a kiss. "We know all about bad men, don't we, sweetie? Brady may have done some bad things, once, but his heart is good. He's certainly helped us. What are we going to do about that, pumpkin?"

Grace pressed her wet rosebud lips against Susanna's cheek as her mother held her.

"Yes, baby, if only all the world's problems could be solved with a kiss."

She knew they couldn't. In fact, kissing Brady had only brought more problems into her life. She squared her shoulders and prepared to go back to work. Heading toward Grace's play corner, she started to put her baby down, but Grace suddenly bucked in her arms. She held out her dimpled hands.

Susanna glanced to where Grace was reaching and saw that the baby had noticed Brady.

"Buh," Grace said. "Buh!" She practically wailed the sound as if her heart were breaking.

At that moment Brady turned. He stared at the baby holding out her arms to him. He looked at Susanna and she couldn't hide her automatic reaction to him. She glanced down, hoping he hadn't noticed the naked desire in her eyes.

"I'm sorry," she said, walking toward him. "Grace gets a bit stubborn when she likes someone."

Her baby was practically crawling out of her arms trying to get to Brady.

He looked down at the baby. Susanna was pretty sure he wasn't the kind of man who had held many babies. Given his loner status, she would consider it a safe bet that he'd never held a baby. She knew he liked the quiet and solitude of his home best.

Grace's lip quivered. She looked at Brady with tear-filled eyes.

He reached out and took her from Susanna, his big hands cradling her small body.

Immediately, Grace smiled and gooed. She settled against him.

"Oh, my," Susanna said. "Brady, I'm so sorry. Here, let me take her back. If I give her something to play with, she'll be fine in a minute."

Brady stared directly into Susanna's eyes. "Have a seat. I'll bet you don't get much time with her during the morning rush. I'm also betting that you miss that."

Susanna nodded. "I do. I was a stay-at-home mom, and it's been hard to not be there for her every minute, even though Lydia has been more than wonderful about letting me keep her here with me. But no, I can't sit. There are still customers."

"Sunny's seeing to them."

"Sunny's a customer herself. Lydia doesn't pay me to sit down." But she wanted to. There was nothing she wanted more in this moment than to sit here and watch Brady holding her child and looking as if he didn't mind at all that Grace was chewing on his shirt. Trent had never liked the mess of having a baby. He hadn't been at all pleased when she had gotten pregnant. It was only after she'd left him that he had professed to wanting to be a father. If he ever figured out where they were and came looking for them...

Susanna realized that she was clutching her apron, her knuckles clenched tight.

Brady glanced at her hand. He reached across and loosened her stranglehold on the cloth, his fingers gently stroking until she released the material. Warmth flooded through her as his skin caressed hers.

"Lydia won't mind if you take a minute," he said. "Things are pretty quiet right now, anyway. The morning rush is over."

Susanna nodded tightly. "Yes, everyone has gone back to their businesses. Do you want...?" She glanced over her shoulder to the door directly across from his new office. Nothing seemed to be going on there. No new sign, no indication that furniture was being delivered or the office was being refurbished in any way.

Something close to an uneasy smile flitted across Brady's face. "Brought my work with me today," he said, indicating the laptop on the table. Grace was trying to reach the keys.

"Oh, you're working," Susanna said, suddenly distraught. He had come here to work and here she was, sitting across from him, letting him be sidelined by her child.

"Well, that's it. I'm more than rested. I'd better get back to waitressing," she said with a big smile, rising to her feet and scooping Grace up, ignoring her baby's squirming attempts to get back to Brady. "Thank you for being so nice to Grace."

She looked at Brady and saw that he really was smiling this time. "You weren't keeping me from work, Susanna," he told her. "I work when I please. I do as I please, and I always have."

He said that as if it were a warning, and Susanna took it as one. What he was saying was true. She really knew very little about the man.

But as she moved to place Grace back in her play area, she passed a table of women she didn't know.

"It's despicable that he should show up here large as life and push himself on the people of this town," one older woman said. "Lon Banks is a good man. He shouldn't have to be subjected to Brady Malone. And all the baby-holding in the world can't change that." The woman gave Susanna a killing look. With some effort, Susanna kept herself from reacting.

Later, when Brady had crossed the street to his new office and the place was empty of all but Lydia and Sunny, who was getting ready to go open up the dairy shop for the lunch crew, Susanna asked about the women in the booth.

"Biddies," Sunny said with some distaste.

Lydia shook her head. "Maybe so, but they're not alone in that attitude, Sunny. I've never had a problem with Brady, but there are plenty that do. You should know that, Susanna."

Susanna bit her lip. "Do you want me to quit my job? I don't want to be the cause of you losing business."

Lydia laughed at that. "Honey, don't even think about it. I just want you to know what you're up against. People may make rude comments to you.

They may say hurtful things, but I don't worry about people criticizing me. Although I have been known to turn away a customer or two, I don't have anything against Brady. If he wants to come back every day, he's welcome. Besides, those women weren't regulars. It's a wild guess, but I'm betting they came here specifically because they heard that Brady Malone had dared to show his face in town lately. I had much more business than usual this morning. On the other hand, if he gives you any trouble at all, he's history at the Red Rose. We like having you and Grace here.'' She gave Susanna a kind smile.

So Lydia wasn't going to hand her her walking papers, but Susanna wasn't fooled into thinking that she had heard the last of the cutting remarks. She'd noticed a few other mean stares cast Brady's way this morning. She only hoped he hadn't noticed.

He had been so good with Grace. He had been good to her. Surely that counted for something. If only the people of Red Rose had a chance to get to know the Brady Malone she had known thus far.

But Susanna knew that if asked, Brady would agree with the bitter women at the table she'd overheard this morning.

How could she change people's minds? Should she try? She'd only known the man a few days.

A vision of Grace nearly in tears because she couldn't get near Brady came to mind. Her daughter was friendly and open about being held, but she didn't cry to be held by just anyone. And Grace wasn't the only indication of Brady's kindness. Susanna remembered the freshly painted garage, the way he'd left food for her that first day, the way he'd fixed her car when he could just as easily have let her be taken to the cleaners by Nate Fisher.

She remembered the pain in his eyes and the way he'd shielded his expression when he'd seen Lon Banks.

There was a lot she didn't know about Brady, but then there was a lot the people of Red Rose didn't know about him, either.

What could she do about that?

Chapter Nine

It wasn't that he wasn't working, because he was, Brady told himself. Some of his work was portable, and he could drag it along with him. He wasn't lying about that part. It was just the other part that was giving his conscience pause.

He had outright fabricated that part he'd told Susanna about expanding his business to Red Rose. He would never do that. That would mean facing his past and his failures every day of his life.

So instead he'd hauled his laptop to town, sat around at the café waiting for her ex-husband to show up and tried his best to keep his eyes off Susanna. He'd almost been succeeding, too, when that sweet little baby of hers had held out her arms. What a cutie. What a tangle.

"This isn't easy, Scrap," he told his dog. "Be glad you get to stay home. It's much safer here."

Scrap lifted his head for an ear scratching and gave

his master a long look that said "I agree with you, buddy. Home alone is best."

But at that moment Brady heard a car pull in the drive.

Susannah, of course, because even if he hadn't been expecting her, he recognized the sound of her engine. Maybe if he retreated back into his study, he wouldn't hear the sound of her walking to her door; he wouldn't envisage what she looked like.

He was just getting up to head to the back of the house when a light rapping sounded on his door.

Scrap gave a welcome woof and rushed to the door, his nails clicking on the wooden planks.

"Traitor," Brady muttered. "If you had kept quiet, she probably would have assumed we were working and gone away." But even as he said the words, he knew he didn't mean them. His breathing was too damn hard. His body was too tense. He was as eager to see Susanna as his dog was.

And so he pulled open the door, looked down at her and prepared himself for that sparkle in her green eyes. Damn, preparing himself hadn't worked. He still felt as if he'd been hit over the head with a giant slab of rough granite. She made him that light-headed. Dressed in that prim little white blouse and black skirt that she wore to the Red Rose, he could still see the gentle outlines of her breasts; he could still taste her sweetness against his tongue just as if they'd kissed only seconds ago.

She was smiling, even though her eyes looked a bit uncertain.

"Hi," she said, and held out a plate of cookies. "Lydia let me use her kitchen again. I think I'm getting better."

He looked down at the cookies as if he'd never tasted one before. "You baked for me again?"

"Hey, I have to have someone besides Grace to practice on," she teased. "You act as if you've never tasted home-baked cookies before."

He hadn't, at least not very often. His mother had spent most of her time avoiding his father and then she had died. None of the Malone males had done more than rudimentary, barely-keep-you-alive cooking. They were too busy lying, cheating, stealing and raising hell.

He wasn't going to say that. Not again. He'd already told her about his past.

"They look tasty," he said, surprising even himself with a smile. "Real tasty. Thank you."

And then she laughed, a pure, lovely sound. He thought he'd willingly walk through fields of flame just to hear her do that one more time. He wanted to be the one to make her laugh, which was, in itself a joke.

"They're a bribe," she confessed.

He raised his brows. "A bribe? For what?"

Susanna cocked her head. "I want to ask you to take Grace and me to the flea market tomorrow." She said it real matter-of-factly, just as if it was the kind of thing people asked of him all the time. As if she didn't know that people didn't invite him places. Maybe she didn't.

Heck, of course she knew. She'd been there today with all that whispering going on.

"You want to go to the Red Rose flea market? Why?"

She shook her head and wrinkled her nose, then looked down at her daughter as if the two of them were sharing a secret. "He wants to know why we want to go to the flea market, Gracie. Because," she said, tipping her head back to stare directly into his eyes. "It sounds like fun. And because I want to pick up a few things for the house now that I have some money."

"The house?"

She tipped her head toward the garage. "Don't you dare say anything mean about my residence now. I just want to dress it up a little. I promise I'll whisk everything away and take it with me when I go."

A flea market. Crowds. Lots of people from four counties. A perfect place for a stranger to hide out without being noticed. If that stranger knew about the Red Rose flea market. If he was smart and savvy, he would know. Susanna had indicated that her ex-husband had managed to get into her house undetected. He had bypassed locks. Sounded like a bully, but not a stupid one.

"I won't make you carry anything," she said softly. "And I won't do typical woman things and make you give me your opinion on colors and stuff like that."

She sounded slightly forlorn, slightly desperate. He wondered if her ex-husband had reprimanded her for doing typical woman things. What an idiot. Any sane man would go out of his way to have Susanna ask for his help.

"Are you always this impulsive?" he asked, and he couldn't help smiling down at her.

Susanna shook her head slowly. "There's nothing impulsive about me. I think everything through very carefully."

Which was why she had headed for Red Rose without knowing a soul and had ended up stuck in front of his house. Being careful explained why she had gone out in the dark of night to plant flowers in front of his house when everyone else knew better than to sneak up on him like that.

She was like one of those flowers she'd planted, soft and slender and very breakable. Someone was trying to break her. He wanted nothing more than to spend the day with her hand on his arm leading him around from booth to booth, and because he wanted it so badly, he knew he had to deny himself. Except…he had sworn to protect her. Nothing was going to stop him from protecting her, not even his own good sense or his pride. Not even the fact that he was sure that people would later whisper things about him into her ear. Things that were true and that she would be wise to believe.

"What time?" he asked.

She rose up on her toes as if she were going to kiss him on the cheek. Heat surged through him even at the thought of something so innocent. He gave her a stern look.

"Don't even think about doing that. It's your lips I want, and you know it. You and I can't trade innocent kisses on the cheek. If we touch at all, I'll take it further. You know that."

She slowly lowered herself, a shy, uncomfortable look in her eyes. Damn, he had made her self-conscious. That hadn't been his intent.

"All right, yes," she said. "I just didn't think."

But of course, she wasn't an impulsive woman. She was a woman who was careful and thought things through, which was why she thanked a man who had a black and ragged reputation by giving him spontaneous kisses on the cheek.

"I'll try not to ever do that again," she was saying. "I can see you're not a hug-and-kiss kind of man, but just so you know, I'm not all that innocent. If you tried to take it further, I might want it, too."

"Might?"

"Do, even if I know it's wrong for me and for you."

Something hot and male and primitive ripped through him, and it was all he could do not to pull her roughly against him, to take her right here in his doorway.

"What...what time?" he asked again, struggling to keep his mind free and clear.

She touched her lips as if he'd actually kissed her. "Nine o'clock?"

"All right. Bring a hat for the munchkin. One for you, too, and lots of sunscreen. You both have that lady-fair skin. A day at the flea market can be more brutal than you think."

She turned to go. He started to let her.

"Susanna?"

"Yes?" She turned back and then he took her by the shoulders. He kissed her hard, his lips searing hers, his body snug against her for just a second, long enough to make it clear to both of them that he needed a very cold shower.

"While we're at the flea market, let's drive out and look at some apartments. Maybe in another town." He practically growled the words.

"You want me gone," she said.

No. Yes. Darn it, no, he didn't, but yes he had to send her away. "It would be best," he said roughly.

"Then I'll start looking right away," she said in that voice that slayed him every time.

And when she had gone, what then? Would he bay at the moon and pine for the mate he wanted but couldn't have? What would he do?

"I'll go on as I always have," he told Scrap after Susanna had gone. "We'll be just as we were before she came with her cookies and her flowers and her soft green eyes and even softer skin."

Scrap gave him a look that told him he was a liar.

"Smart dog," he told his pet. "I wish you were smart enough to tell me where her ex-husband is. I have the feeling he's not just sitting around content to let her go. I'm afraid he might be getting closer."

Susanna had never been to a flea market. She hadn't been to much in the past few years when Trent had always made excuses to keep her at home. And, honest to Pete, she hadn't come to this flea market with any idea of enjoying herself. Not really.

It was just that Sunny and Lydia and Joyce and Tommy and her other friends at the Red Rose Café had talked as if everyone showed up now and then at the "market," as they called it. And it was just that she figured that if she came with Brady and forced people to actually get to know a little about how he conducted himself, then surely everyone would see what a good and worthy man he was. Good heavens, the man was trying to expand his business into Red Rose. How was he going to do that if half the town thought he was a reincarnation of the black knight?

She glanced up at Brady who was pushing Grace's stroller and looking like a man who was out of his element. His military-short, dark brown hair and erect posture marked him as a very masculine man used to all male companions and superior control. The utter disarray of the flea market was anything but controlled; the pink bow tied to the handle of Gracie's stroller was anything but masculine. He should have been uncomfortable. And yet when he caught her staring at him, he gave Susanna a long steady look that ended with her being the one in need of composure.

"Anywhere in particular you want to look?" he asked in that low gritty voice. "Do you know what you want?"

She wanted security, a home for her and Grace. She wanted friends and warmth and safety. Brady didn't have any of that to offer, but then he wasn't talking about those kinds of things, was he?

Susanna took a deep breath. She looked around at the colorful stands and tables. "A lamp," she said with some conviction. "A home needs light and warmth and color. I'm looking for anything that will give us that. A lamp for starters."

"Lots of those here," Brady remarked. And yes, there were tons of them piled everywhere. All different colors and styles from many different eras. For a minute, knowing that Brady was studying her, she couldn't concentrate. The tables and booths of lamps mingled in a dizzying swirl of brass and wood and ceramic bases and cream colored shades. But then she forced herself to pretend she was unaware of the man beside her.

"That one," she said, pointing to a small table with just a few items.

"The one that looks like a lighthouse?" he asked with a trace of amusement in his voice. "Were you a sailor in another life?"

"I can barely swim," she confessed. "But even though I like the lighthouse, that wasn't the one I meant. I prefer the one that looks like a little cottage surrounded by pale green grass and flowers, with the square lampshade. It's just what Grace and I need."

Brady studied her openly and with intensity, then pushed Grace's stroller over to look at the lamp. "You're right. It suits you. It's delicate, the kind of thing that belongs in a warm, homey place. And there are those flowers again." He picked up the lamp and stroked his thumb over the textured petals of a ceramic rose. "How much?" he asked the seller.

"Oh, no," Susanna said. "I didn't bring you here to buy things for me."

"Fifty dollars," the man behind the table said. "As you said, it suits the pretty lady."

Susanna reached for her purse.

"Thirty," Brady said, putting his hand out to stop Susanna. But she was so surprised to hear the amusement in his voice that she had already stopped looking for her wallet.

"Thirty? That's robbery. This is a genuine Damien Crewe," the man said with a wounded look. "I could never take thirty."

"Damien Crewe?" Brady said, looking to Susanna. "Are you a big fan of Damien Crewe?" His voice had dropped, becoming low and sexy and conspiratorial. He was half laughing, and she was charmed.

She looked up into his blue eyes. "I don't know. I've never heard of the man," she whispered.

"She's never heard of the man," Brady said, giving the seller a pained look. "You can't ask a person to pay extra for an artist that no one has ever heard of. Thirty."

The man bristled. "Forty-five and that's a blasted bargain."

Brady turned as if he meant to walk away.

"That's it?" the merchant growled. "No bartering?"

Brady shrugged. "I'm just going to ask a few people here if any of them who come here all the time know who Damien Crewe is or if you always use that line on those of us who aren't regulars." He stepped out into the crowd. He started toward a group of people.

"Sir," he said to a man, and Susanna could just imagine him using that tone of voice to a fresh recruit. "Mind if I ask you a question?"

"All right! All right!" the merchant yelled. He muttered something about ignorant yokels, but in the end he agreed to take thirty for the lamp.

Susanna hid her smile as Brady conducted the transaction, but when they had moved on to the next aisle of goods, she smiled up at Brady.

"You are really bad," Susanna said to him as they walked on.

He shrugged. "I know."

"I meant that as a compliment. Do you really think there is a Damien Crewe?"

"If there is, I'm going to feel real guilty in the morning, but I suspect it's just a sales tool the man uses on everyone."

"I would have paid the fifty."

"You need your money. You have a baby. She's going to need things as she grows up."

But of course Brady wouldn't be around to witness Grace's growing years. As if he'd just thought of that, too, he grew silent. The squeak of the stroller's wheels mingled with the noise of the crowd. Susanna knew she should call attention to herself and Brady. If people saw how good he was with Grace and how kind he was to escort a woman and baby around the flea market when he had a life of his own to live, they might rethink their old opinions of him.

But it was so nice just being together, the three of them, that she couldn't move into action just yet.

"Ah, here we go," Brady said, pulling up in front of a table.

Susanna looked down. Spread in front of her were the most beautiful creamy-white cotton blankets embroidered with dainty flowers. Blue forget-me-nots, yellow daisies, pink rosebuds.

"They're gorgeous," she said.

"I thought you'd like them. You seem to have a thing for flowers." Brady reached into his pocket and gave the lady at the table some money.

"Oh, no, I can pay," Susanna said, panic rising inside her. She hadn't brought him here so that he could buy her things. Warmth rose up her neck into her cheeks.

"Let me," he said. "You gave me flowers. I'm just returning the favor."

Indecision and guilt warred within Susanna. She had asked him here for a reason. How could she let him pay her way?

But the look in his eyes stopped her from saying no. This was a man who had faced roadblocks all his life. People had doubted his motives and turned away from him. She couldn't do that, too.

"Thank you," she said softly and let him drape the blanket around her shoulders. Just then she looked down at Grace and saw that her daughter had fallen asleep.

"Oh, my," she said.

"She looks uncomfortable," Brady replied and, without another word, dropped to one knee and unstrapped the baby from the seat belt that held her in. He gently lifted her into his arms, then handed her over to Susanna. When she had Grace snugged against her body, he rearranged the blanket, brushing at her hair that had gotten caught under the edge.

"I'll get you home," he whispered.

"Well, isn't that cozy?" a voice called out. "Brady Malone and his woman. Maybe his baby, too. Those Malones never could do anything right. I wouldn't be surprised if he'd left a slew of illegitimate babies over half the county, him and his brother and his no-good father."

Susanna sucked in a breath. She could feel Brady stiffen at her side, and she turned to look at the man who was talking even though she didn't have to look to know who the voice belonged to. Nate Fisher stood there, his big belly hanging over the edge of his sagging jeans, a sneer on his face. When her glance connected with his, he laughed.

"I hear you got a husband," he said.

She knew she should just ignore him, but she couldn't seem to help herself. "Ex-husband," she replied, her voice cracking.

"Probably heard that you were hanging around with a Malone."

Susanna felt herself go cold. This man didn't look a thing like Trent, but his words and actions were much the same. All she'd wanted when she came here was to get away from all that, and yet she hadn't.

"Let's go, please," she said to Brady, but he wasn't looking her way.

Tall and strong and rigid, his expression hard, he turned and started toward Nate Fisher.

"Brady, no," she said, but he didn't answer.

"You can say what you want about me, Fisher," he said as he neared the man and kept advancing. "You can spread your venom to the winds." He took another step toward the man, backing him up against a table.

"For myself, I don't care," he continued, pushing forward, so that Nate Fisher fell back against the card table, sending an array of goods crashing to the ground along with his own meaty frame.

Brady stood over him, his hands in hard fists as he held his ground. "None of that makes any difference to me," Brady told the man, "but if I ever hear you saying one negative comment aimed at Susanna or Grace, I will smash you into the ground so deep you'll come out on the other side of the world."

And with that, he gave one apologetic look to the merchant, reached into his wallet, pulled out a sizable wad of bills and handed it over, then walked back to Susanna and gently shepherded her and Grace away from the crowds.

He looked like a man who had just buried his best friend, and so Susanna didn't speak as they climbed into the car. She gave him time to recover from what had just happened. They were almost all the way back home when he slowed the car and turned to her.

"I'm sorry about that," he said quietly. "You didn't get to finish your shopping."

He said it so matter of factly, as if shopping really mattered to her, that she didn't even think. She just opened her mouth. "I didn't go to the flea market to shop," she confessed.

He raised a brow. "Why did you go then?"

She turned away, furrowing her brow. "I went there because I was worried about you."

"You were worried about me." He said it as if she'd just spoken in Japanese and he didn't understand the language. "Why would you be worried about me?"

Susanna crossed her arms over her chest and gave him a stubborn frown. "Oh, I don't know. Maybe because you always tell me how bad you are. Maybe because I wanted people to know that you weren't that way. You're good with Grace," she insisted. "You're kind to me. I wanted people to see how wonderful you are."

"I see," he said, and then he didn't say any more.

"Brady?"

"Yes?"

She looked at him. His jaw was tight, his hands lay easy on the steering wheel, but he didn't look happy or at ease in any other way.

"You're not mad at me because I lied to you, are you?"

"What do you mean?"

"I mean that I told you I was going to the market to look for things for the house, and instead..."

He sighed. "Instead you had some sweet but misguided plan to make me look like a choirboy. I'd say it's you who should be angry with me."

"I am, a little," she said in a small voice.

"I don't blame you, but I told you all along that I was not the kind of good man you thought I was. Me and your ex-husband..."

She quickly turned in her seat. "Don't ever say that."

"What?"

"What you were going to say. You and Trent are nothing alike. He pretended to be good and turned out like...well, a lot like Nate Fisher. You're not like that."

"All right, maybe I'm not as bad as that, but I'm no choirboy, either."

"I know that."

"That's why you're mad, isn't it? I'm sorry, Susanna."

"That's not why I'm mad."

She had his attention now. He slowed the car, pulled it to a stop at the side of the road. "Why are you mad then if it's not because I messed up your plans and added fuel to the gossip's fire."

"I guess I'm mad because you didn't stick around and let me applaud. No matter what anyone else thought of what happened back there, I'm grateful for what you said to Nate Fisher. I would have said so, too, if you hadn't looked like you were in such a hurry. And I'll tell anyone who asks me that you had good reason to hit him, even though you didn't lay a hand on him. You might not be a choirboy, but you're a good man to have around when the bullies roll into town, Brady."

"I have a temper," he argued.

"You controlled it."

He shook his head. "I seem to recall having to pay a sizable chunk of money to that merchant."

"It wasn't your fault that Nate Fisher backed up and knocked everything down. And it definitely wasn't your fault that he said all those nasty things."

"I knew it was a risk escorting you around in a public place."

"It's a risk I chose to take."

"And it backfired."

"I suppose. I guess the gossips of the town will have a field day with this one."

"They will. For Grace's sake, you need to keep your distance from me."

"I want Grace to know that she shouldn't believe everything she hears. I want her to learn to judge people for herself."

"Susanna, we were in a public place today, and I nearly hit a man."

"But you didn't."

"I wanted to."

"Not the same thing."

"I told you that I'm no choirboy. You don't know what you're getting into."

She had to sigh at that. "I'm not getting into anything. We've both agreed that we don't want to get involved. And just for the record, I never did think that you were a choirboy."

"No?"

"No. Choirboys don't kiss like you do. I know. When I was twelve, Billy Talbott kissed me in the back pew of the church. He was a very good boy, and it was a nice kiss, but it wasn't anything like the kiss you gave me."

And that was all it took to keep Brady awake half the night. He didn't have a clue what kind of kisses Susanna had received in her life, and he didn't know what kind of men she'd encountered other than her no-good ex-husband. What he did know was that he wanted to kiss her lips again. He wanted to slip over to her little box of a house and make love to her beneath a white blanket covered in flowers. He wanted to make her cry out with passion and need.

But he wouldn't. If he did, he would be playing right into the lies that Nate Fisher had told. He would be acting like a typical Malone, and for once in his life, he wanted and needed to do the right thing. Susanna and Grace were at stake and he would never do anything to risk their happiness.

Even if it meant that he had to lie awake aching for all the long hours until the dawn.

Chapter Ten

The whispers got louder that week, Brady couldn't help noticing, as he resumed his visits to the Red Rose Café. More people, both women and men, crowded into the booths, and soon he was wondering if he was doing Susanna any kind of a favor. Maybe the town had just settled into the summer doldrums and the good citizens needed something to keep them occupied. For whatever reason, he apparently looked like this week's entertainment, and Susanna was kept jumping to keep all those people fed.

Moreover, since the incident with Nate Fisher, many of the curious or condemning glances were cast her way rather than just at him. Obviously the world now knew that Nate had hinted that Susanna was Brady's bedmate and some came here just to gawk.

"Don't pay any attention to them," Rosellen January said to him that first day after the flea market incident. "They're just jealous because nothing exciting ever happens in their lives. The women wish they had a man to stand up for them, and the men, few as they are, wish they had the guts to do the standing up. I think it was pretty admirable.''

Brady looked up from his coffee. Rosellen had gone to school with him. He couldn't remember ever having had a conversation with her.

He shrugged self-consciously and went back to his coffee. When he had been in the service, he had accepted his promotions as his due. The military code was exact, and he understood it. Here he was out of his element. He hadn't grown up receiving compliments. He wondered what Susanna had been telling the ladies of the town. He had a bad feeling that she was painting him as some kind of hero.

But before he'd had a chance to think about that too much, Susanna was at his side. ''Looks like you're working hard,'' she said, a teasing note in her voice.

He glanced in the direction of her gaze. His laptop was open on the table. The screen was blank. He'd been sitting here for an hour.

Damn, caught!

Brady lifted one shoulder in dismissal. ''I do lots of work in my head.'' Which was true much of the time, but not today.

''I didn't mean to pry,'' she said. ''I used to think I wanted to be an artist, and a lot went on in my head before anything went down on paper.''

He couldn't help but stare into her pretty green eyes. ''An artist?''

She blushed a most becoming shade of pink. ''Well, I never actually accomplished my goal. It was mostly a dream.''

He reached out and covered her hand with his own.

"I wasn't making fun of you. I never would. What was your medium? Sculpture? Glass? Paint?"

"Mostly paint. Landscapes. Some real, some imagined. I wanted to create my own worlds. I love the way things fit together to make each place unique in a landscape, whether it's a real world or one that's pure fantasy."

Landscapes? He could see that. Susanna standing on a hillside or beside a lake, the wind catching in her hair as she concentrated on her canvas or the vision in her head, the woman more lovely than the landscape she wanted to recreate.

"You gave it up."

She attempted a smile. "It wasn't practical."

Somehow he knew those words weren't hers. He had a feeling they were her ex-husband's.

"Everything in life doesn't have to be practical," he said gently. "Sometimes when I get tired of inventing some purely utilitarian piece of software, I amuse myself by creating a game or two. It's a release."

Her eyes grew big and excited. She raised one brow and grinned.

"Brady Malone playing games? I almost don't believe it."

He wanted to laugh with her. "Believe it."

"Could you show me? You have some on your computer?" She looked down at the slim black case.

"One or two." And suddenly he wished he'd spent more time creating frivolous games, just so he'd have something to make her look at him this way.

She leaned closer. "I was going to ask if you wanted to accompany Grace and me on a picnic at the edge of town. I can't keep her cooped up here all day, and most days we take a break midday just so Grace can get some fresh air. Would you do that, and would you show me what you've made?''

A picnic at the edge of town, right where everyone could see her with him. That wasn't anything like these mornings at the café, her doing her job, him a paying customer. Going out alone together socially might make people start whispering about her. She was new to town and a woman alone. She needed to be careful, to get a good start with the right people, like the ladies of the café, not him.

He started to shake his head. "I don't think that's a good idea.''

Instantly her smile dimmed. She pleated her apron between her fingers. "I'm sorry. Of course, you have work. I guess I wasn't thinking.''

She thought he didn't have time for her or that he didn't want to go on a picnic with her and that sweet baby. "I don't want to steal your private time with Grace,'' Brady said. It was partly the truth, but mostly he didn't want to steal what she was making for herself here in Red Rose. A good place to live with no whispers following her around.

Susanna looked toward the other room where her baby was being entertained by two ladies. "You know that Grace loves spending time with you.''

He did, and that was another reason why he should keep his distance. He did not want that baby being hurt by gossip or speculation.

"And I'll feel safer knowing that there are two of us watching over her.''

Well, what was he supposed to say to that? "What time?'' he asked.

"As soon as the breakfast crowd clears.''

And that was how Brady found himself sitting on a faded plaid blanket beneath a tree in Red Rose Park, not fifty feet from the baseball field where he'd once sat on Junior Denhopper's head and demanded that he take back the bad word he'd said about Brady's mother. It was where he'd once been arrested for underage drinking. Right now it was where he faced Susanna with Grace between them. Susanna was slicing a coffee cake and handing him a piece on a plate from the café.

"Too late for breakfast, too early for lunch," she said by way of apology.

Didn't matter. The food wasn't exactly the draw in this situation. The woman with the shining eyes and the baby clapping her chubby hands together were the main attractions.

He ate his coffee cake, even though he hated coffee cake.

"Show me your creations," she said, looking toward his laptop computer. And for the first time in a long time, Brady felt self-conscious. Reluctantly he pushed the computer close to her and tapped on the keys. The game that came up was of the role-playing variety, white knights and black knights. She gazed at him in astonishment.

"You gave me this idea," he said, and he showed her how to play.

"It's wonderful. It's…it's noble, even romantic," she said a few minutes later when the game had trounced her.

Brady shrugged. "It keeps me out of trouble."

Susanna got a fiery defensive look in her eyes, and Brady chuckled. "I was teasing, Susanna. Really."

She looked a bit flushed, but she finally smiled a bit. "Okay, you were teasing. You're forgiven then."

He felt a glow that he probably shouldn't have felt. He tipped the computer closed, preparing to take her back to the café. But when he started to get up, she touched his shoulder.

"Let's walk, all right?" she said. "I love this place, don't you? It's so…so small-town America." And she started to stand.

He rose and took her hand, helping her up. He picked Grace up and placed her in the crook of his arm.

"I guess it is," he said, even though he had never loved this place. There were some boys, maybe nine or ten years old, playing baseball in the dusty field. They reminded him of his own less-than-stellar childhood. They looked so young and carefree and all that boys that age should be. One of them, the littlest one, was holding the bat as if it were a frightening instrument of torture.

"My heart goes out to him," Susanna said. "I loved baseball, but I was always rotten at it."

"He'd be fine if he just had a bit of instruction," Brady said. "And if his companions stopped hassling him. I'll bet he's more self-conscious than anything."

Susanna gave him a speculative look. "I'll bet if someone was around who knew the least little thing about how to hit a ball, that someone might give him a tip or two."

Brady couldn't help his smile. "How often did you tell me that you came here?"

She didn't even blink. "Most days."

"These boys here often?"

"Um, most days. It's summer, you know."

He gave her a long look, an amused look. "It won't work, you know, this campaign to make me look better than I am."

Susanna opened her eyes wide, feigning innocence and ignorance. She stepped close and gave her daughter a raspberry kiss on her bare pudgy leg. Gracie giggled. "It wouldn't hurt you to just give him a pointer or two. And Grace would be so proud of you."

Brady laughed out loud. "I'll bet you envisioned some wonderful paintings. You have a most vivid imagination, Susanna. And all right, I'll offer my pitiful services, if it will make you and Grace happy. Just don't be surprised if the kid turns me down and spouts a few choice words at me. Most boys that age don't like having their shortcomings pointed out publicly." He never had, even though he'd been terribly aware of them.

Susanna touched his arm. "Like it or not, your shiny silver armor is showing, Brady."

He almost swore, but then he remembered that he was holding a baby. Gently he lowered Grace into her mother's tender arms. He indulged himself by fluffing the baby's silky blond curls. "Your mother is an optimist," he told her.

Grace cooed and kicked in agreement.

"Mind if I join you?" Brady asked, sauntering up to the boys.

The scruffy group of boys, stained with dirt and grass turned toward him. Their expressions suggested that he might have just grown antennae and descended from a cloud.

"Not supposed to talk to strangers," one boy said.

"He ain't a stranger. That's Mr. Malone," another boy said in wide-mouthed awe.

"Double ain't supposed to talk to him. Malones are no good," the first boy said. Brady heard Susanna gasp but he let the comment roll off of him.

Most of the boys started to turn away.

"You could maybe be on my team for a minute or two," the small boy who had been unable to wield the bat told Brady. "I bet we'd win then. I bet *you* could hit something. Catch, too."

"I bet you could hit something, too, if you just adjusted one or two things you're doing," Brady said.

"Nah, I'm hopeless."

"Nah, you're just fighting the bat. No need to. It's a part of your body when you're playing baseball, like an extra arm. Use it like it belongs to you, like it's something that you sleep with and eat with and live with all the time. It's just an extension. Here, let me show you." He stepped up to the boy and tipped the bat slightly. "'Scuse me, boys," he said to the rest of the crowd. "My teammate and I just need to consult for a moment."

Susanna watched from a distance. She had Grace to watch out for, and besides, this was pure guy stuff. She was afraid the boys would be self-conscious if she got too close, and that wasn't what she was aiming for.

What are you aiming for? she asked herself, and there was no point in denying the truth. Brady had been right about her scheming. She hadn't exactly planned the thing with the boys as he'd suggested, because she had asked him on this picnic without thinking the whole thing through. Still, she had hoped that a good moment or two might come of this day.

People would see Brady helping a woman and her child, acting like any other good man out on a picnic.

He *was* a good man. He was good with the boys. Even the one who had been standoffish was watching Brady with interest, and the little guy with the bat phobia had finally managed to connect with the ball. Not gracefully or powerfully, but did that really matter?

"I hit it. I hit the ball," the boy called, jumping up and down, almost forgetting to run to first in his excitement, and Susanna couldn't help noting the pleased smile on Brady's face as he said goodbye and bowed out of the boys' game.

"Satisfied?" he asked Susanna as he came back to her side.

"Ecstatic," she agreed. "Hi, Mrs. Jarvis," she called, waving to a woman walking past the park.

The woman stopped in her tracks. She stared at Brady, suspicion in her eyes. Then she nodded to Susanna.

"Told you that you couldn't rewrite history," Brady said, leaning in close to whisper in Susanna's ear. A delicious shiver ran up her. She was instantly aware of him as a man, and she turned to face him.

"There will always be people who don't see the truth," she said. "Besides, there will always be people who do see the truth. Here come Tommy and Annie Winterbourne." And Brady turned just as the two women appeared.

"What a great day for baseball," Thomasina said. "You appear to be a fine teacher, Mr. Malone. An admirable pastime."

Brady angled his head. "Good morning, Thomasina, Annie. You picnic here often?"

Annie, who owned Annie's Curls for Girls, gave him a big smile. "We don't picnic, but Tommy and I walk here. Every single day at this time. I've been watching that little boy try to hit that ball for days. I was beginning to think he would give up. I'm glad that you were able to help him."

The two women said their goodbyes and walked on.

When they had gone past, Brady turned to Susanna with a speculative look. "Did you set this up?"

She hid a smile behind her hand. "You act as if I asked you to rob a bank instead of show a boy how to hit a baseball."

He focused on her then, intently, his dark blue eyes never leaving her face as he reached out and stroked one finger down her cheek. "If you try to play guardian angel with me, Susanna, you'll only get hurt. There are things you don't know about me, some things that no one knows about me."

"I know what I see, and what I see is good."

"You married a man who wasn't good. Yet, I have to believe that at one time, you were mostly blind to his flaws."

Susanna froze. A hint of pain and truth pricked her. She struggled to maintain her composure.

"I'm sorry. I should never have said that," Brady said, frowning angrily. "That wasn't even close to fair. I don't know anything about your past and your marriage. I just…"

"You just wanted to warn me that you are trouble. You just wanted to protect me," she said as she walked with him out of the park and back to the café where he left her at the door and went back to his office.

For half the day she reflected on his words. He was right. She had been blind to Trent's flaws, but there was a difference. At first, Trent had wanted her to see only his most positive side. If he had hidden the truth and his true nature from her, it hadn't been out of some bid to protect her, but to fool her.

Brady's words had cut, but they had backfired on him, because knowing that he was trying to protect her from himself only made her care for him more than she already did.

Maybe he was right. She should stay away, but what a woman knew she should do and what she actually did weren't always one and the same thing.

So what exactly was she going to do?

Chapter Eleven

All evening long Brady played the scene in the park over and over again in his mind. Susanna was on a mission of some sort, and he had hurt her. He cursed himself for that stupid comment about her ex-husband. No matter how much he wanted to convince her that he wasn't what she thought he was, he had no right to hurt her by trying to drive her away.

If he really wanted to protect her, if he really wanted her to see the truth, then he had to tell her the truth. She knew part of his story, but she didn't know all of it. He had never told all of it to anyone but Davis, and that had been on a lonesome night when both of them had had too much to drink. He didn't want to tell Susanna the ugly facts of his past, either, but like military discipline when a soldier had erred, some things just had to be seen to.

And some things had to be ended before the world came crashing down.

So the next morning he stuck around the café instead of going across the street to his empty office where he could observe people going in and out of the Red Rose Café at a distance, which was what he had been doing for the past week. Today he waited for Lon Banks to come in, to force the confrontation he'd been avoiding for too many years.

Susanna couldn't help noticing Brady. He usually didn't stay this long.

"That man certainly has the hots for you, hon," Sunny said when Susanna passed by her table.

Susanna felt distress climbing her chest. She had tried her best to pretend she hadn't noticed Brady's prolonged stay this morning, but she had been more aware of him than ever. She had spilled coffee three times and had almost dumped a full plate of eggs and sausage on Mercy Granahan's lap. She didn't want to be so aware of Brady, but she just couldn't help it.

"He's just working, Sunny," she said.

Sunny gave her one of those what-pea-patch-were-you-born-in? looks. "Lady, that man sits here every morning, and every time you walk by, he practically has to chain himself to the chair to keep from touching you. That isn't work he's concentrating on. That's a man lusting after a woman, and believe me, hon, I know what lust looks like." She smiled at the man seated across the table from her.

Chester Atchison looked up from his paper and reached out to stroke Sunny's neck. "She knows about a lot of things, Susanna. Believe me, if she says the man wants you, he wants you."

But Susanna already knew that Brady wanted her. Wanting a woman physically just came naturally to a man, and there sure wasn't any doubt that she wanted

Brady that way, too. What woman wouldn't? But that wasn't why Brady was here today. Every morning since he'd made the decision to bring his business to town, he'd had his breakfast here. This was the first day he had stayed. Something was going on. She didn't think it had anything to do with her, but she was the one dropping the food.

Finally, when it was almost time for her to take a break, she walked up to Brady.

"What's wrong?" she asked.

"What makes you think anything is wrong?"

"You're still here, and you don't look as if you want to be here."

He studied her carefully, then he looked around the room. "Do you know Lon Banks?"

Oh, no. The man Lydia had told her about, the one who had given Brady the hard look. "I know who he is."

"I thought he usually came in here."

He had. Before that day. "I guess he isn't coming today. Did you need to talk to him about something?"

Brady shook his head. Then he did what he'd never done before. He reached out and touched her arm. Publicly. "Come with me. I need to talk to you about something. Will Lydia watch Grace, do you think?"

"I'll see." She knew that Lydia would, or that someone trustworthy would. But Susanna needed a minute to compose herself. Brady had said that they needed to talk. He hadn't sounded happy, either. Maybe he was going to ask her to leave and find a new place for her and Grace to live. How was she going to feel about that?

She didn't know or…well, yes she did know. The pain gathering in a lump in her chest was proof enough that she was growing to care for this man too much.

"I'll be right back," she said softly.

Two minutes to compose herself, another two to talk to Lydia, one to shed her apron. She wouldn't comb her hair or check her makeup. That was what a woman did when she was going to meet a man she was in love with, a man who actually loved her back or who at least might love her one day in the future. That wasn't going to happen with Brady.

He wanted to talk. It couldn't be good.

She slowly walked to his side. He rose and took her hand and led her from the café. "Make sure you bring her back safe and sound, Brady," Lydia called.

Brady turned and exchanged a solemn look with the owner of the café. "I won't keep her long," he said quietly.

And then they were on the street. They walked down the main drag, a row of pretty little buildings with a feminine touch. Storefronts with railings along the sidewalk trailing ivy. Flower boxes filled with white and blue and pink flowers. Everything was clean and neat and welcoming and sunny. Susanna should have felt good.

Instead she looked up at Brady's troubled expression.

"Where are we going?" she asked.

"To see a man."

"Anyone I know?"

"You'd recognize him. Lon Banks."

"You don't have to do this, Brady."

"Yes, I do."

"I already know about your brother and Mr. Banks. Lydia told me."

"She must not have told you enough. Maybe she doesn't even know all there is to tell you. If she had, you wouldn't be trying to convince the world that I'm a better man than I am. You wouldn't be encouraging everyone to think that I'm some sort of hero for losing my temper with Nate Fisher the other day. I've had several people thank me for that, so I know you must have told them. That isn't right, Susanna. You're seeing things in me that aren't there."

"You make me sound like some sort of dewy-eyed girl. You know I'm not that."

"Maybe not. I know life, or at least a man, has treated you harshly. That ought to have made you more cautious."

"It has."

He stopped and looked down at her. "Not with me."

She shook her head and touched his sleeve. "Even with you. I *am* cautious in a way I don't want to be. I know that I have to be careful."

"I don't think you're as careful as you think you are."

"I don't think you're as bad as you say you are."

"If you don't think so, then look." He had stopped in front of a glass-plated window. Everything about the building was neat and clean and precise. The lettering on the window said Lonnie Banks, Attorney-at-Law.

"I don't understand." Susanna frowned. "I've walked past here many times."

"Look at that sign, Susanna. The man is a lawyer. A fine job for some, but a lawyer wasn't what Lon ever wanted or intended to be. He was young once and vibrant and extremely talented. He could hit a ball fast and clean and sweet, right out of the park. He could run the bases and slide into home, dodge a fielder if he had to, dancing away from the tag. He was something to watch. He was on his way to a sure-thing college scholarship playing ball until my brother drank too much, climbed behind the wheel of a car and ran him down.''

He said the words as if he had been the man driving the car.

''That was your brother, not you. You were young. Everyone said so.''

''It was more than that. Do you know why Lon went into law?''

She did, of course, but she didn't want to say the words, so she merely tipped her head in assent.

''Tell me what you know.'' His words were cold, as if he were accusing her of doing something wrong. That made Susanna angry, because she knew what he was doing. He was trying to make her turn away from him.

She raised her chin. ''He went into law because he couldn't run or play baseball anymore. Is that the correct answer, Mr. Malone?''

''It's the answer most people would guess, and it's partly right, too. But maybe no one told you the rest of the story. Maybe they don't even know. Lon lost the full use of his body that night, run down by a drunk driver, but the evidence against my brother wasn't as compelling as a prosecutor would like it to be, and so Frank got off with a slap on the wrist. They needed more evidence.''

Brady stared directly into Susanna's eyes then. He reached out as if to take her by the forearms, but he stopped just short of touching her. He stood straight and tall, an anguished look on his face, the planes of his face hard, the depths of his eyes as sad as she had ever seen a man.

"I knew Frank was guilty, Susanna," he said slowly. "I overheard him talking to my father about what had happened. I knew the truth, and yet I didn't tell a soul. I think Lon's always suspected that."

The searing pain passed from Brady's expression into Susanna's soul. "Frank was your brother," she whispered.

"There was no love between us. I could have testified against him. I could at least have given Lon that."

"Why didn't you?"

Brady didn't answer. He just stared at her for long moments. "It doesn't matter. The point is that I'm not a hero and I don't want to be one. And for the record, that business with Nate?"

"Yes."

"I'm afraid it may have cost you. I didn't want you to know this, but I have some reason to believe that your ex-husband has been looking for you. I thinks he's been asking questions on the town's Web site."

Panic surged through her. "Why didn't you tell me?"

He looked away, and then he turned to her and gently stroked one finger down her hair. "I didn't want to scare you. I had Lorelei, the Web mistress, try to lead him astray, and I set up my own roadblocks, also trying to lead him away from you. I wouldn't be telling you now, but…"

He sighed and blew out a frustrated breath.

She touched his hand, which brought his gaze back to hers.

"What's happened?" she asked. "Why are you telling me this now?"

"Because I don't trust Nate," he told her. "I didn't want to tell you anything. I had hoped I could head your ex-husband off, but I don't think that has happened, and I want you to be more careful from here on out. If I should look away at the wrong moment or not be there at just the right time when you need help…"

"I can't ask you to be responsible for me."

"You haven't."

"I don't want you to feel like you have to take on the burden of me and my child."

"I don't feel like that."

But she knew that he had a greater than normal sense of responsibility. He couldn't walk away from a woman and a child who had no one else to protect them.

"I thought maybe…when you called me out here…maybe you were asking me to leave."

"I wouldn't do that."

Of course not. He wouldn't do that, because if he asked her to leave, then he couldn't guard her and Grace. And if something happened, he would feel the weight of guilt and responsibility pulling him beneath the water. Again. Just as it had when he was a boy and his brother had ruined Lon Banks's life, and he had kept the secret. His brother had gotten off with a light sentence, and then Davis had died, making it impossible for him to render restitution for the wrong he'd done. Since then there had been no one to take the blame except Brady, and he was still blaming himself.

He had lived with regret all these years, and he never wanted to regret anything again. So Brady would always do the responsible thing. He would take care of her and Grace.

Even if he didn't really want to.

"You should go back now," he said. "I'll walk you back."

"No."

That brought his head up. "Why no?"

She slowly shook her head. "I came here on the run, Brady, prepared to move on as often as necessary. But the longer I stay here, the more friends I make, the more I realize that I really came here to find a place to make a home, to take a stand and stop running, to get away from all that. No matter how much you might want to, you can't save me. Only I can save me. And I don't want you to even try."

Anger rose in his blue eyes. "If you think I'm going to stand idle and let some good-for-nothing man push you around—"

"That's not what I meant. If it came to a test of physical strength, I would welcome your help, but I don't think it will. And there comes a time when a woman has to stop and take her life back if she thinks she's lost it. You and Red Rose have given me the courage and the incentive to do that. You gave me back my lost self-esteem, so this is where I stop running. This is where I stand. I'm moving out this weekend, Brady, because I have to do things for myself now. You can't stop me. So please...be good to yourself. Please just be free."

And she reached up and placed her hands on his

shoulders. She rose up on her toes and kissed him lightly on the lips.

He shivered beneath her touch.

She pulled away slightly and waited. "Your turn," she whispered. "Tell me goodbye, Brady. Do it."

He slid his hands beneath her arms. He splayed his palms across her back and tugged her against his hard body. Slanting his head, he brought his lips down on hers and tasted her. He brushed her with heat and need and hunger, and she opened for him eagerly.

He kissed her again. "Tell me to stop," he whispered against her lips.

"No. I want this."

His arms tightened around her. "Think, Susanna, do you really want this?"

She did.

"Here, on a public street, when you know it's not going anywhere?"

And that was all it took, his admission that this *was* just a physical attraction. Of course, she couldn't have that. She had a child. And while she might chide him for an overactive sense of responsibility, she wasn't really being fair, because she had responsibilities of her own. She had to think of Grace.

Stepping out of his embrace, Susanna tried to steady herself. She tried to smile up at him. "You ought to bottle that stuff and sell it at the flea market," she said with a shaky voice. "You're one great kisser, Brady Malone."

And then she turned to go.

"Don't go yet," he said, his voice laced with need and steel.

She stopped and looked over her shoulder. "I can't stay. If I do, I'll only hop back in your arms, and we both know that would be a mistake. Besides, I have work, a baby to support.''

"That's not what I meant. I meant…don't…don't leave the house. Not just yet. Just let me…''

"Make sure I'm safe? I don't think I can do that. Taking care of me is killing you. I can see that now.''

"You're wrong. Taking care of you is a blessing, a privilege, an honor. I'm trained to protect, Susanna. Let me do it.''

What to do? She didn't want to be his responsibility. That was far too painful to contemplate. She didn't want to even think about how he would beat up on himself if Trent even got close to her. But she *did* have a child to consider, and Brady *was* trained to serve and protect.

She gave a tight nod. "If it comes to that. How long do you think it will be before he finds me?''

"Not long. Lorelei told me this morning that she hadn't gotten rid of him completely, if the man who was asking questions, is in fact, your ex-husband. And now that Nate has an ax to grind…well, Nate is mean, but he's not as stupid as he looks. And he's mad. He'll want revenge. He knows you're my soft spot now. And I happen to know that Nate is an Internet addict. Sooner or later, he and your ex-husband will make the connection.''

Susanna felt faint. She worked to hold herself erect, but she should have known that Brady would notice the change in her demeanor.

"I won't let him near you or Grace, Susanna,'' he promised. "I've failed people before, but I give you my word, I will not fail you.''

Tears pooled at the backs of her eyes. She had to leave or let him see how deeply he affected her.

If Trent got near her and Brady missed it, Brady would never forgive himself. She loved him too much to let that happen.

She loved him. Oh, how she loved him.

And loving him, there was only one solution. She had to end this thing with Trent once and for all. And she had to make sure that Brady saved her, and that everyone knew it.

That was going to mean she might have to put herself in some small amount of danger. And that was what she intended to do, just as soon as she ensured Grace's safety.

When she left Brady's home, she was going to make sure that he was free of any guilt concerning herself and her daughter. When she left Red Rose behind, and she knew now that she would have to, the town was going to know that he was the best of men.

The man she was going to love forever.

From afar.

Instead of going directly home that night, Susanna stopped in at the library and asked the librarian if she could use their computers to access the Internet.

She looked at the list of social activities Lydia had told her that the town had scheduled, and she picked out what seemed to be the most promising. Then she laid her fingers on the keys and sent her message. She hoped that she was doing the right thing for her baby and herself and for Brady.

Chapter Twelve

Brady had been on his computer for hours. He had used every skill he possessed, did things that were most likely illegal, but in the end, he had what he wanted, proof that Nate Fisher was trying to harm Susanna and more important, Brady had finally ferreted out the identity for the man who used the screen name Justice. He even had some idea of where Trent Wright had posted from these past few times, though he'd been moving around.

And now with Nate's help, Trent appeared to be practically right on Susanna's trail.

Brady needed some way to smoke the guy out, to get him to show his true colors. Then he intended to teach the man something about true justice. He would use the law or whatever means were necessary to make sure Susanna was safe from this bottom feeder.

He typed a few words into his computer and waited.

While he was waiting, an announcement was added to the town's electronic bulletin board.

This wasn't a message, and it didn't need any deciphering or any advanced knowledge of the electronic arts. Just a simple, one-sentence addition.

Susanna Wright has volunteered a box lunch for the Red Rose Community Church Social this Sunday. The box lunch auction for this and all other donations by the ladies—and some men— of the town will begin at noon. All serious bids will be accepted, and the proceeds will go to fund a new church library.

Brady roared. He all but kicked the computer table across the room.

"What the hell does she think she's doing, Scrap?" he asked on a groan. "Doesn't she know he's out there looking for her?"

Of course she did, and she knew this would bring him to town. In a sense, he could almost understand her actions. What must it be like to be hiding from someone all the time, to sit around waiting and wondering when and where that person would show up and shatter everything good in life? And what must it be like to fear for your child every minute of the day? No wonder she was coming out of hiding.

The fact that he had been the one to tell her that Trent was close to finding her and that he, therefore, was the reason she had made herself a bull's-eye on a dart board scalded him, flayed his soul.

He had thought she was at risk before, but he was the one who had put her at risk.

"And I'm the one who's going to take care of

things,'' he told his pet. ''Get into battle mode, Scrap. The day after tomorrow is the church social, and you and I are going hunting.''

As if he knew what his master had commanded, Scrap rose and stood proudly, waiting.

''Do you think this is wise, Susanna?'' It was mid-afternoon on Saturday, and Lydia sat at the table across from Susanna, frowning. For once the café was empty, and it was just the two of them. ''Trent sounds like a man who likes power. By letting him find you, aren't you giving him too much of that? Men who feed on bullying others aren't easily controlled. What if things get out of hand?''

Susanna pressed her palms against the tablecloth to keep her fingers from shaking. ''I know it's not wise, Lydia, but do you honestly think it's wise to let a man like that ruin the rest of my life? I'll never **have** peace until he's stopped, and I'm hoping that if he confronts me in a public place this time, I'll have legal recourse to take steps to keep him away.''

''And if things get physical and ugly?''

''Trent's never hit me. He prefers the humiliation method of control,'' she said. ''But if he did try to hurt me, I could use that against him, and I would. I've gotten back some of my self-esteem since I've been here, and I'm not giving it back easily.'' She laid her hand over Lydia's. ''You've helped me a great deal. You've been a friend as well as **an** employer.''

Lydia smiled. ''It's easy to be a friend to you, but I'm pretty sure you've always made friends easily. What I'm guessing hasn't been so **easy** is finding good, true men to take away the taint of the bad ones. Does he know?''

Susanna almost said who, but she wouldn't insult Lydia that way. ''He knows about Trent. I haven't told him about the Sunday social, but I know he'll find out and he'll be there.''

''Why didn't you just tell him?''

Susanna gave Lydia a look of disbelief.

''I suppose you're right,'' the older woman said. ''He would have just tried to stop you. He would have been right to do that, too, but I guess it's your life, and no one but you has the right to manage it. Just so you know, there are going to be a whole lot of us standing between you and your no good ex-husband come Sunday.''

''I was pretty sure you'd be there,'' Susanna said. ''Thank you.''

''Joyce is going to keep Grace?''

''Yes, the two of them seem to have formed a special bond, and I trust Joyce implicitly.''

Lydia nodded. ''Joyce always wanted children, but she just never found the right man. Maybe someday…but for now, I know she adores your baby. She'll keep her safe while you do what you have to do.''

At that moment the door opened slowly, the bell above it clanging softly, as if a light breeze had come through. But it was not a breeze standing in the doorway.

It was not even a regular customer.

Susanna looked up, straight into the eyes of the man she'd once thought she knew, the man who had taken all the dreams she'd ever had and crushed them into the ground.

Her heart began to thud wildly. She wanted to run, but she could do no more than rise, so quickly and awkwardly that the chair tipped and clattered to the floor. She pressed her hand to her chest. The urge to run to her baby was great, but she wouldn't do that. Trent hadn't noticed Grace sleeping in the playpen in the corner of the next room, and as long as he didn't notice her, Grace might be all right.

She opened her mouth to speak but nothing came out.

Her ex-husband laughed, an oily sound that suggested that he enjoyed her discomposure. "You thought you could leave me, Susanna, and I would just let you do that?" He shook his head. "Not gonna happen. You married me for better or for worse. Doesn't matter if you thought it was all worse. Not your choice to make. Consider yourself lucky that I'm willing to take you back. Look at you," he said, staring at her apron. "Working as a waitress when I gave you a six-bedroom house with a swimming pool? You're a joke, Susanna."

At that, Lydia started to step forward, but Susanna cut her off with a small slash of her hand. There was something in his eyes that suggested that things had gotten worse. A glassiness. Susanna wasn't completely positive what it meant, but she was pretty sure that Trent might be taking drugs, and if that was true, then he could be unpredictable. And she would not allow anyone to get hurt protecting her.

"I think this is between Trent and myself," Susanna said, hoping Lydia understood. "You can go, Lydia."

Trent shook his head. He laughed again. "Not going to happen, wifey mine. She leaves that door, who knows who she'll go to? In fact," he said, reaching back, flipping the Closed sign to face the window and pulling the shade down over the door, "I think it would be best if I just make sure that your friend here doesn't talk to anyone when I take you out of here. I meant these for you," he said, pulling two looped ropes from his pocket, "but I figure you're going to come with no argument. This lady, now, I need to subdue."

"Trent, no. Please!" Susanna said, holding out her hand. "Let's just go now, you and me. I'll go with you right now."

"You think I believe that it's as easy as that? You think I'd let you leave without your daughter, knowing you'd try to get away as soon as we were out of town? Uh, uh. When you leave with me, you leave for good. Now tell me, my dear wife, just where is Grace?"

Trent smiled.

What have I done? Susanna thought. What have I done, and more important, what am I going to do?

Get away, she thought. Somehow get away with Grace as fast as possible. And pray with all her heart that no more of her friends, especially not Brady, discovered that Trent was in town.

Because she firmly believed now that she had been mistaken earlier when she'd told Brady that Trent was not violent. Under the influence of whatever he'd taken, he was most definitely capable of violence. And if he and Brady came face-to-face, blood would be spilled. She'd heard that some drugged individuals developed superhuman strength. If Brady came here....

"I'll take you to Grace," she said, and she moved toward the door. "If you want the two of us, let's go now."

Brady had been sitting in his chair, facing the window of the café, his feet propped on an old footstool he'd brought in, his computer on his lap. He'd brought Scrap with him today, and his dog lay on the floor carefully gnawing the choicest bits of a bone. If a small bit fell on the floor, Scrap lapped it up neatly with his tongue. His dog had manners.

As for the dog's master, he was a basket case today. Brady acknowledged that fact. He'd spent the morning watching the door of the Red Rose, but most of the morning patrons had gone. Somewhere inside Susanna was still there.

"I don't like this setting herself up as a sitting duck, boy," he told Scrap. "If I knew where this guy was, I'd make a preemptive strike. As it is, sitting here pretending to work when I know he's after her is making me feel pretty useless."

Scrap looked up from his bone as if to concur.

And then Brady noticed the door to the café closing. Someone had gone in while he was turned toward his dog, and he had missed it.

"Darn it, Scrap, don't let me do that again." He leaned forward, straining to see past the lacy curtains that Lydia had in her windows. He could just see a man's back, Susanna turned toward the man, her face not giving away a thing. She rose as if to wait on a customer and then she looked toward Lydia.

The always-composed, always-tough mayor and owner of the café wore a look of impotent rage. Her brows were drawn together and she held her body stiff. She took a step forward, then stopped.

"Something's not right," Brady said. "That's got to be him, and if it's not him, it's not Santa Claus, either."

His suspicions were confirmed at just that moment when a hand reached back, flipped the Closed side outward and pulled down the shade on the door.

"Let's go," Brady yelled, and he and Scrap both tore toward the door and clattered down the stairs. Brady had faced men bigger than he was, he'd faced men with less fear and more muscle. He had once or twice in his army days, stepped into barroom brawls where life more than honor was at stake, and he had once been cornered in a dark alley by two men wielding knives. Never had terror raced through his body as it did in this minute.

Susanna had eluded her husband for weeks. She had done her best to escape his clutches, and then she had all but mocked him by placing a public announcement of her whereabouts.

Now he was here to get her, and there was more than one door to the Red Rose Café.

"Look out!" Brady yelled, banging his hand on a car coming down the street as he and Scrap dashed in front of it. Man and dog cleared the remaining steps in two seconds flat, and Brady rammed his shoulder against the café door, flinging it open.

Stepping into the shaded interior, he saw Lydia's dead-white face, Susanna with fear and determination in her eyes, and a man wearing a white shirt and tie with a pair of navy pants. The man's hair was slicked back, immaculate, not a hair out of place. The scent of expensive cologne wafted from him; a Rolex was clasped around one wrist. But when Brady looked into his eyes, he saw nothing resembling an appreciation of life. This was a man who liked to call the shots, who liked to own things, and right now he was reaching out to clasp Susanna's wrist.

When Brady moved, the man clamped down on her skin hard and pulled.

"Sorry, restaurant's closed," he said with a small smile that didn't reach his eyes. "Come back tomorrow."

Brady took a step that carried him one step farther into the room and also blocked the door. If the man was going to try to drag Susanna out of here, he would have to get past Brady.

"I don't think I *will* come back here tomorrow," he told the man. "What I want is here today."

The man looked at Susanna and gave Brady an ugly, speculative look. "What exactly do you want?" he asked, taking his other hand and raking it across the pale skin at Susanna's throat. Brady could see her swallow. She was trying not to show her fear, but he knew it was there.

"You want her?" the man asked. "Why? She's nothing. She's just a waitress. She dropped out of college her first year. Did she tell you that? She couldn't cut it. She thought she was an artist, but she didn't have any talent. She's not even all that pretty when you look at her closely. Too skinny, too angular. She's nothing without me," he said, and Brady could tell that it was a phrase the man had repeated many times both to Susanna and to himself.

He wanted to look at Susanna, to tell her that the man was lying, but he couldn't take his attention from the man. Watch your target, he told himself. Don't ever lose sight of your target.

"Since she had the baby, she's even gotten paler,

her skin sags in places,'' the man continued. ''You should see some of those things she painted. What a joke!'' he said with a sneer.

And despite the fact that he was starting to zero in on this jerk, Brady couldn't ignore the woman. To hear him talking about Susanna that way....

''Don't listen to him,'' he told her, his eyes never leaving the man. ''He's wrong.''

She was silent for too long. He took his eyes off the man for half a second and the guy gave a tug. Instantly, Brady was almost on top of him. Almost but not quite. Trent still held Susanna. He could still hurt her.

''You all right?'' Brady asked, barely able to find his voice.

He heard her drag in air. ''I'm...fine,'' she said, her voice coming out a bit wispy. ''Really, I'm fine. And I'm not listening. I'm good. I'm okay with this. You should go. This is between Trent and me.''

Some part of him that he'd thought couldn't be hurt screamed out in pain, but he knew enough of verbally abusive relationships to know not to trust what he was hearing. Moreover, he knew enough of Susanna to know that she would try to save everyone from any perceived danger, even if it meant standing up to that danger herself. She might have been cowed by this man once, but she had guts and she was learning to fight.

''I'll go soon,'' he promised, but he took a slight step forward, making no attempt to leave.

''You don't want her. She's nothing,'' the man repeated, and this time he made a quick sideways move, swinging Susanna in front of him, her arm twisted behind her back.

Somewhere in the café, a clock was ticking. Outside Brady heard someone come by, look at the Closed sign and continue on. The angle at which Trent Wright was holding Susanna's arm was surely painful. In the background, Brady heard a slight movement, a tiny gurgle.

The baby, he thought, staring directly into Susanna's eyes. She had appeared distressed before, but now she looked practically frantic.

Brady forced as much calmness on himself as he could muster. He made himself look directly into the man's glassy eyes, claiming as much of the guy's attention as could be claimed.

"You're right," Brady said, rising from his slightly crouched stance to a more relaxed pose. "I don't want her. I want you. Around, Scrap," he said, and his dog circled to the right, blocking the door and lunging at Trent Wright's exposed side.

The man jerked and turned slightly, and Brady rushed forward, taking advantage of his momentary lapse to pull Susanna out of his grasp and nudge her toward Lydia.

Now it was just him and the scumbag.

The man laughed. "Big guy, but not big enough I'm afraid. I've studied martial arts for years," he said. He lunged forward, catching Brady in the neck with the side of his hand.

Brady nearly went down, and he heard Susanna and Lydia gasp. For half a second he saw bright, raging red. Susanna had said that her ex-husband had never physically abused her, but he could well imagine that the man's mannerisms might imply the threat of physical violence, even if a woman was almost certain the man wouldn't carry through on the threat. This man was one of those who liked to issue threats. He liked to have others subservient. Brady felt a surge of pride in the woman he loved. She had taken her baby and gotten out, and she had not allowed this man to win. It gave Brady a renewed sense of strength and purpose.

He rubbed at his neck, feigning more pain than he felt. Pain was nothing. His father had beaten him regularly, his brother, too, with bare fists or with anything that was close at hand, no matter how hard or sharp the object. It was why he'd never told the truth about his brother and Lon, because he was pretty sure neither his father nor his brother would hesitate to beat him senseless. He had had no one in the world to protect or to care about him, and there had been times as a boy that he had wondered if dying wouldn't be better than living. But after the accident, he *had* been afraid of dying, of the payback his brother would mete out if he talked. He had been scared, more than scared then, but he wasn't scared now.

"Martial arts?" he asked roughly. "You've studied martial arts for years? Well, I haven't." Not for a while, anyway, even though he had once studied it carefully and with great purpose. He had excelled, too. If he wanted to, he could use all that skill against this man today. He could beat him that way, most likely easily. But he didn't want this to be easy or neat. Or civilized. Especially knowing how uncivilized this man had been to Susanna, how he'd mistreated her, how he'd terrorized her and Lydia by coming here today.

"You don't know martial arts? I thought not. You yokels aren't that refined," the man said, and he raised his chin, preparing to make his next move.

"I do know this, though," Brady said in as soft and low and cold a tone as he could muster. He brought his fist up hard and fast, smashing it into Trent Wright's jaw and sending him crashing backward into a table. "Basic army tactics in a tight corner," Brady said just before he picked the man up and hit him again. "Works pretty well in most circumstances. You're going to be wishing you'd never come here when tomorrow morning arrives. You're going to wish you'd never come near Susanna, and if you ever come near her again or threaten any woman in this town ever in this lifetime—" he said, planting his fist in his opponent's face one more time. "I'll show you what I *do* remember of martial arts." And he dropped the man to the ground.

The man lay there groaning for several seconds. Then he shoved himself to his hands and managed to lean against a nearby wall.

"There's more than one way of winning," Trent said, his voice thick around his swelling tongue. "I know all of them, and I have people who will be willing to testify that I came here to see my daughter and that you attacked me. Influential people who will have alibis placing them here at this place and time, people who can ruin this café, bring down the owner, bring down as much of the town as I want to bring down. I can do that, and I can win. A respectable businessman ought to be able to come into town without fear of being savagely attacked. I'll hold the city council and the local police personally responsible for not protecting me. Red Rose is going to be sorry they sent you," he said to Brady. "You just touched the wrong man."

Susanna stepped forward, her eyes blazing. "You don't have any witnesses," she said.

Her ex-husband gave her a withering look that said she was amazingly naive. "Susanna, my dear, you know that I can do pretty much anything I want to. Believe me, my witnesses will trump yours. Next time, don't send a ruffian to do the job." He slowly rose, brushed himself off and moved toward the exit, turning when he reached the door. "You haven't seen the last of me, Susanna. After this, I'll be more determined than ever."

"She's seen the last of you," Brady said, "because if you ever come near her again, no matter where I am, I'll come back and find you and make you wish you'd never even breathed her name."

Trent bristled with barely contained anger. His entire body shook and his eyes glared hatred, but he didn't answer. Instead he turned and stormed out of the café.

When he stepped out into the light, a crowd had gathered, most likely brought by the sound of crashing and the oddity of having the café closed and shaded in the middle of the day. "A disgrace," Trent said to the crowd. "That man is a monster that shouldn't be allowed in your midst. He attacked me. I assure you that if this were my town, I wouldn't allow him to stay."

Some of them cast accusing eyes Brady's way. They nodded to Trent.

Brady wasn't concerned with them. "Are you all right?" he asked Susanna and Lydia, and because he couldn't help himself, he gently ran his hands up and down Susanna's arms where her bullying ex-husband had bruised her with his grasp.

"I'm fine," she whispered, joining in Lydia's assent. "You?"

"I'm good," he said, even though he lied. He had brought trouble to Lydia and the town. Trent Wright was just the type of man to relish a lawsuit and some old-fashioned revenge.

"Grace," Susanna said, but Joyce Hives had come up with the baby. "When I saw the Closed sign, I came in through the kitchen. Brady was beating the pulp out of the guy and little Grace was waking up, so I whisked her out of sight. I've called the sheriff. He's on a call, but he'll be here soon," she promised.

"I'm sorry," Brady said. "Lydia…"

She raised her hand. "Don't worry, Brady. He needed a beating, and I don't believe he can do what he says he can do."

Susanna didn't look so certain, but she touched Brady where Trent had chopped him on the neck. She ran gentle fingers over the spot. "Are you okay?" she asked. Then when he nodded, she gave him a sad smile. "Thank you."

He shook his head. "I know what you were doing. I saw the notice on the Web site. I'm only sorry I brought so much grief to the town. Most likely I should have called the law."

Lydia shook her head. "He would have already dragged her from town. She would have gone in order to protect all of us. I'm not worried, Brady. The town council has a lawyer. He'll sort this out. I'll tell him the truth."

Brady's breath stuck in his chest. "Lydia, you mean Lon?"

"He's a good lawyer," Lydia reasoned.

"I'm not doubting that," Brady said, "but I think

you have to reconsider the situation, Lydia. A Banks is not going to get involved in a lawsuit where a Malone is the defendant. Isn't that right?'' Brady asked, and he turned to the crowd. He had seen Lonnie Banks there among the rest. Now the man came forward.

"I'm committed to justice," Lon said, his words slow and reluctant.

Brady looked into the man's cool eyes, the same eyes he'd been seeing for years. "I know that," he said, "but be honest. You really wouldn't want to have to defend me, would you?"

For long seconds Lon said nothing. Then he looked to the side. "You're most likely right. Wrong or right, just or not, unreasonable or not, some things haven't changed. I don't feel comfortable around you, and I don't think I ever will."

"That's not fair," Susanna said, rushing forward. Brady held out his hand to stop her, but she shook her head vehemently and kept moving toward Lon. "I wasn't around all those years ago when the Malones were doing whatever the Malones did. I know that's true," she said, her voice heavy with emotion and indignation. "I can't feel what you felt when you watched your dreams slip away, at least not in the same way it happened to you. I realize all that, but…"

She looked at Brady. "I also realize that Brady is not the kind of man who would sit by and let a person be hurt without trying to help. He just wouldn't."

She was shaking. Brady stepped up behind her. He gently placed his hands on her arms and held her. He leaned his head down close to hers. "But I did, Susanna. When I was young…things were different. I was different. Things weren't the way they are now.''

Lon studied the two of them. He wasn't a big man, but he looked as if he had a big weight on his shoulders. ''You're right. Things were different then, because Brady was only thirteen when Frank plowed into me. Frank and Asa Malone would have beaten Brady to a bloody pulp if he'd come forward to rat on one of them. Everybody knew that. We all knew Brady was a scared and confused kid. It isn't Brady I've been battling all these years,'' he said, and Brady wasn't sure if the words were for him, for Lon himself or for the gathered crowd. ''It's not Brady I've been fighting,'' Lon admitted, ''but my own disappointment at having to give up everything in life I wanted.''

''And that's something that can't ever be changed or made right,'' Brady said. Susanna was still now. He released her gently and stepped away. And then he signaled to Scrap and walked out of the café and down the street.

He could barely think, barely function, he didn't want to feel, but he was feeling plenty. His throat was closing up quickly, so he turned just once and looked back.

''Susanna,'' he called, and she started toward him. He quickly shook his head. ''He said he had connections. Well, believe it or not, I have a few, too. Still. Army buddies don't forget the past. I want you to know that you don't ever have to worry about him hurting you again. I'll make sure you're protected.''

And then he left just as fast as his car could carry him. He figured if he threw just the basics in his car, some clothes, his computer and some food for Scrap, he could be gone in half an hour.

He could be somewhere else in no time. This was the last gift he could give her, this town that was more hers than his, anyway. She could have a place all her own, one where she might be able to make that dream true to life someday. She could paint, she could find a good man, she could make more sweet little babies.

Life would be good for her.

He prayed that life would always be good for her. And he hoped that if he left, that jerk would focus on him and leave her alone.

Chapter Thirteen

"He's gone," Susanna said, her heart shattering as she watched Brady climb into his car and drive away. "He's leaving."

"He'll be back tomorrow, honey," Joyce said. "He always shows up for breakfast."

Susanna shook her head. "I don't think he's coming back. I think he's leaving town. That thing about his army buddies…the lawsuit…"

"The last Malone in Red Rose gone." Someone said the words, a sense of awe in the female voice.

To Susanna's relief no one did what they might have once done. No one said good riddance. Which was a good thing, because if one person had said one bad thing about him, the tears would have slipped down her cheeks. She was barely holding them in as it was. She had come here in search of a life and lost dreams, and now the dream she hadn't even known existed had just walked out of her life. And there was nothing she could do to convince him that he was the right dream for her.

Instead she turned to Lon, who was looking sad and tired. "I'm sorry about your lost hopes," she said quietly. "I—I know you won't want to believe me, but... I know that Brady is sorry about that, too. Maybe more sorry than any one of us here. He's lost a few dreams of his own, hasn't he?"

Lon studied her with solemn gray eyes. "I suppose that's true. He wanted an army career, didn't he? And he lost a good friend in that accident."

"He doesn't talk about it much," she said.

He nodded. "He wouldn't. I never talk about my accident, either. Too painful, too big. But then everyone who has to let go of a dream thinks their loss is larger than life, don't they?"

"I suppose they do." She stared off in the direction that Brady had gone.

"I wonder if I would have ever become a lawyer if I hadn't been injured," Lon mused. "I wonder if I would have met my wife and had my kids if I had gone off to play for the big leagues. I love my wife and kids beyond belief," he said, and Susanna turned to see him staring at Grace who was cuddling in her mother's arms. "Maybe I did get my heart's desire, just not the one I started out with," he suggested somewhat sadly.

Tears filled Susanna's eyes. She tried to nod at Lon, but was afraid that she would break down right here in front of everyone. He was trying to do the right thing, trying to move on and offer an olive branch. He was suggesting a way that he and Brady could live together here in relative harmony.

She hoped they could. She wished she could be a

part of that, too, but it didn't change some things. Brady wasn't going to let her be a part of his life. He was a man who had given up dreams because they had never come true for him. And sometimes not having a dream was better than having one and losing it.

There was a rustling and shifting in the crowd. "You say that Brady's leaving town? It seems like a shame to just let him go that way. I was getting used to seeing him in the café all the time," someone said.

"Yes," another person said. "And the way Lydia said he stood up to that man who was threatening her and Susanna, well, it wouldn't be right for us not to have the chance to thank him properly. Brady's been a part of this town all his life. People were just starting to get to know and like him."

"Absolutely. Someone ought to tell him that. Someone really ought to get up the nerve to go after him and do just that." This last voice came out of the midst of the crowd, but it was very familiar. Susanna looked up and gazed into Sunny's encouraging eyes.

She turned and saw that more people were watching her. Waiting.

"It probably won't be easy," one person said.

Rosellen January growled. "Well, do you think that running from a deranged ex-husband and starting out again in a strange town was easy? Susanna knows about doing things the hard way."

"She does," Lydia said softly and with affection, "but if you're going to go find him, sweetie, you might want to hurry. If Brady really is going, he probably doesn't have a lot of stuff he wants to take with him."

Susanna prayed that Lydia was wrong but knew

that she was most likely right. She turned to her friend and nodded. "Watch Grace?"

"She'll be here, safe and sound when you get back."

Susanna hadn't questioned that. Not like she was questioning what she was going to say to Brady. "Thank you," she started to say, but at that moment, Sunny cried out. "Hey, what in heck is Nate doing? Where's he heading off to in such a hurry? Never knew Nate to hurry anywhere."

Everyone turned to look.

"He's headed out of town, and he was on a cell phone."

"Must be an emergency tow."

Sunny growled. "Since when does Nate care about anyone else's emergencies?"

Susanna's heart was climbing into her throat. She was already running toward her car. She half-turned and gave Lydia one last look. "Brady told me that Nate was helping Trent. Something's not right."

"And Nate left on the road to Malone Woods," Evangelina said. "Sounds like he's up to no good."

"Maybe Trent, too," Sunny said. "Well, come on, all of you. Those two may be headed for Brady's. Are we just going to leave him to deal with them alone?"

"Not if I can help it," Lydia said, amidst a chorus of angry voices. "Come on, Lon. You can ride with Susanna and me. We might need some male assistance. Wait up, Susanna."

Fear gripped Susanna's heart. Brady was a strong man, but against two men set on revenge? "All right," she said in a choked voice. "But…hurry."

Everyone sprinted for their cars. Lydia fastened the

baby in the car seat and hopped in as Susanna and Lon took the front seat. Turning the car toward Brady's, Susanna drove as fast as she dared with passengers and her child in the car.

There was a whole convoy of cars behind her, all headed toward Brady's place. Susanna tried not to think about the fact that Brady's home was only two miles out of town, and that he had been gone several minutes before anyone had realized anything was wrong. Nate had been burning rubber. Taking the right roads, he could have made it to Brady's house first.

"Everything's probably all right. Maybe Nate just thought of something he had to do, hon," Lydia said, patting Susanna's back.

"Sure, sometimes things just come up," Lon agreed.

"That's probably it," Susanna lied, but her teeth chattered when she said it. It was nice of them to try and comfort her, but it was far too coincidental that Brady had just beaten Trent at his own game and now Nate, who had good reason to hate Brady, too, was speeding out of town on the road to Malone Woods.

He's going after the man I love, she thought. If she didn't drive fast enough…

Suddenly they were there. Susanna stopped on the grass, but Brady's car was nowhere in sight. She pressed her hand to her mouth. Had Nate and Trent gotten to him before he arrived?

She stumbled from the car, Lon right behind her while Lydia stayed with Grace. The rest of the cars were pulling in, but Susanna didn't wait. She saw Nate's car on the other side of Brady's house and ran in that direction.

She had expected something bad, but what she found caught her by surprise. Nate and Trent were kneeling by the side of the house. Nate was passing a gas can to Trent, preparing to open another one he was holding. Frantic barking was coming from inside the house.

Out of the corner of her eye she saw Brady moving swiftly from the woods, running toward them.

"Susanna, get back!" Brady called, but at that moment the crowd surged forward toward Nate and Trent.

"Don't worry, Brady, we'll help you handle these slimy snakes," said seventy-year-old Donald Orkney, who rarely left the town limits.

"Yeah! Get those two, everyone!" gentle Delia agreed, and the crowd of people who had gathered moved toward Nate and Trent. Susanna noticed that Lon was near the head of the pack.

"Just let me get a piece of that Nate," one woman cried. Susanna realized it was a woman who had been gossiping about Brady only last week. "Brady's a good man. We're not about to let you torch his house." She rushed toward Nate and Trent, who had turned to run but found themselves surrounded.

"I think…" Brady's voice broke, and he looked over the heads of the crowd straight into Susanna's eyes. "I think you have them where you want them. I…thank you, but I don't want anyone getting hurt."

Sunny laughed as she sat on Nate and pinned him to the ground. Lon had Trent's arm bent up behind his back much the way Trent had bent Susanna's arm earlier. "Oh, don't worry about us, Brady," Sunny said. "We're just glad we could save your home. Aren't we, Lon?"

For the first time Susanna saw Lon grin. "Most fun I've had in years," he agreed. He looked at Brady. "Can't have anyone burning this fine man's house. Brady's our neighbor."

Brady blinked, and Susanna's heart gave a lurch. It was going to be so hard for Brady to get used to people liking and respecting him.

"No, we can't have that," someone else agreed. "Brady's one of us. Not like these two. Somebody get a cell phone and call the sheriff so he can lock 'em up. The legal system doesn't take arson lightly, does it, Lon?"

"Not at all," Lon said. "With all these witnesses, I can guarantee that they're going to go to jail for a while."

The crowd let out a cheer. Brady looked around his yard, filled to overflowing with people he had known all his life, people who were calling him champion when they had always called him much worse.

He kept his eyes on Susanna, and her heart filled as he opened his mouth to speak. "I...thank all of you—that is... I wish..."

He turned and walked away into the woods.

A silence fell over the crowd. "Well, are you just going to let him get away, girl?" Evangelina asked Susanna. "The man is headed off to who knows where, and we can't really blame him. We spent all his life criticizing him, and that's not the kind of thing you can wipe away quickly. We'll have to spend a lifetime making up for all the chances we've missed to appreciate him, but I don't think *you* want to wait a lifetime just trying to get close enough to tell him how you feel, do you?"

Susanna turned and looked into Evangelina's eyes.

"No, I don't want to wait. Not one more minute."
She turned and sprinted in the direction Brady had
gone as another cheer went up from the crowd. In the
distance she heard the sirens as the sheriff hurried
over to pick up Nate and Trent.

But there was only one man she was interested in,
and he was moving away from her.

Could she ask him to stay? "Yes, but if he still
wants to go, if he needs to be alone the way he likes
things, then you have to let him," she told herself.
"Or maybe…he isn't the one who should go. If he
needs to be apart from me, I'll go. This is his town."
But the thought of leaving Brady made her throat feel
thick with denial. Her eyes ached with unshed tears.

And then she was there, and so was he, in a clear-
ing in the woods. She stopped.

"Susanna?" he asked.

For two seconds she just stood there, gazing at him,
leaning toward him, nearly teetering.

"Susanna," he said again, softly this time.

And she launched herself into his arms. She slid
her hands up the stubble-roughened planes of his lean
face. Her lips found his and she kissed him with all
the love and passion and longing that was inside her.
She pressed against him, and for several long seconds
simply savored the feel of his body against hers, the
wonderful feeling of being with him.

He was returning her kiss, angling his body to get
closer to her, standing with legs planted on either side
of her, his arm roped around her back. He lifted her
and kissed his way down her chin, to her throat.

It was too much for her, too wonderful. She wanted
more of him, she wanted all of him. She wanted him
to be forever hers, but that just wasn't possible.

With the greatest of reluctance, she planted her hands gently against his chest.

He raised his head.

She stared directly into his eyes.

"What you did back there, what you inspired people to do…it was amazing," he said.

She shook her head slowly and touched his lips with her fingertips. "I didn't inspire them. You did, with what you did to Trent back in town."

Brady frowned. "All I did was get into a fight. Again."

"You protected Lydia and me. You acted when others would have simply watched. And you've done more. I'm guessing that someday Lon will tell you how he feels, but it seems he doesn't miss those old dreams that much because his new ones are so much better."

"I didn't do that for him."

"You made him realize the truth. And can you even begin to realize what you've done for me? When I came here, I was lost, floundering. You made it possible for me to start a new life, to be more than I ever thought I might be, to find depths to myself that I didn't know I had. I—thank you," she said as she lost her battle with the tears that spilled down her cheeks.

"Susanna, no," he said, his deep voice cracking. He leaned close, sipping at her tears. "Don't cry. Please don't cry."

"I'm not," she lied, but neither of them laughed at the obvious fib. "You were going to leave town, weren't you?" she asked.

"Yes, it's true."

"It's because of me, isn't it?"

He didn't answer. Instead he just looked at her with eyes filled with regret. Susanna swiped at her own eyes. "I hoped to stop you from going, but I can't. I just hope that wherever you end up, that, like Lon, you make some new dreams, too, and that they come true. But I really don't think you need to go. This is your home. You have friends here now...and what would Scrap think?"

Her voice failed. The tears came harder, even though she tried to blink and stop them from flowing.

"Susanna, please..." Brady stepped toward her. She knew he was going to take her into his arms, and if he did that...if he did that...

She turned and whirled. "I have to go now. I have some things to do." She ran from him, down the steps, around the groups of people, and back to her little house. She shoved through the door and moved to the small suitcase she had brought with her on that first day.

Because she realized now, that though this had been home for the past few weeks, she couldn't stay here now. At least not in this place. This was Brady's. His soul was here, the evidence of his passing in the new paint and the furnishings and the creamy-white blanket with the flowers. When she breathed in, she breathed in Brady, and if she stayed here, she would be miserable. She had to get out, to find a place in town. Maybe Sunny would put her up for a few days, or maybe Lydia. She didn't know, nor did she care. All she knew was that she had to run again.

But she had barely found her suitcase and started

throwing things in it when Brady came through the door.

"I don't want you to have to leave," he said, coming up behind her.

"I can't stay." She tried to stem the flood of tears again.

And he went to her. Gently he took her in his arms and turned her. "Look what I've done. Are these tears for me? If they are, Susanna..." His deep voice shook. He opened his mouth to start again, and so she forced herself to look up into his eyes, through the mist of pain that almost blinded her.

"You are not to feel guilty about me," she said, her voice as firm as she could make it. "You aren't to blame for my tears in any way, do you hear me, Brady? If I was stupid enough to fall in love with a man who didn't want me, a man who told me repeatedly that he was not looking for a relationship, a man I knew I would be a fool to fall for, then it most certainly isn't your fault. I've been through a lot in my life, but I've learned one thing. I can be strong and I—and I alone—am responsible for my emotional state. So don't you dare feel sorry or feel guilty about me. Don't you dare." Her voice grew stronger at the end and she punctuated her words by poking him in the chest.

"I'm a strong woman, and I don't need anyone," she reiterated.

"You are the strongest of women," Brady agreed. "And you love me," he added, his voice filled with wonder.

"Of course, I love you. Did you think I wouldn't? How could I not love you?"

To Susanna's amazement, a smile lifted Brady's lips, a full, firm smile, the kind she'd never seen on him before. It transformed his rough face. He was magnificent, he was beautiful, he was wonderful, but she barely had time to register those thoughts before he leaned over her and his lips claimed hers.

"You are the most wonderful woman I have ever known," he whispered against her lips. "So, you think I should stay here in Red Rose?"

She nodded slightly, and the exquisite sensation of her mouth brushing his made her swallow. It made breathing difficult, talking almost impossible.

Somehow she managed. She pulled back slightly. "I believe you should try to stay, because I think Red Rose needs you. I think that if you leave, a lot of people are going to have a lot of regrets. I think you should do what you said you were going to do and really open an office in town this time, not just one that you pretend to open."

"You figured that out, did you?"

She closed her eyes. "You were pretty transparent, coming to see me all those mornings in the café, never actually moving any furniture into your office." Remembering all of that, her heart nearly broke all over again.

"And if I stay, what will you do? Will you stay, too?" he asked fiercely, his hands gripping her forearms.

She swallowed hard and touched his cheek. "I—I don't think I can, Brady."

He turned his lips into the palm of her hand and kissed her. "You can do anything," he said. "You're a strong, independent intelligent woman. You can leave your home to save your child, and you can talk an idiot of a man who never helped anyone into turning his life upside down and helping you. You make people feel good about their whole day just with the few words and the smile you give them with their morning cup of coffee. More miraculous than that, you and you alone can turn a black knight into a white one." And with that, he kissed her palm once again, then slid to one bended knee in front of her. "Stay, Susanna, please stay, love."

Susanna looked down at the man who gazed up at her; her soldier, her warrior, her heart. He had called her his love. Joy filled her. She gazed down at him, but she had to be sure she was right about what he meant.

"You want me to stay on as a tenant?" she asked.

Brady growled and tugged her down beside him, seating himself cross-legged and taking her into his arms and onto his lap. "You know that's not what I meant at all, but...yes, I want you to stay here," he said, throwing out his arm in a wide gesture that included all of his land.

And she leaned forward and kissed him on the underside of that rugged square jaw. "I'll stay," she agreed. "But now that you're so popular with the ladies of the town, this property might be more popular. There might be a rush of women wanting to live here. You could raise the rent if you wanted to."

"I don't want to. I only want you, and I think instead of rent, I might change the terms. I think that your name on a marriage certificate and my name on your lips would be payment enough."

Susanna looked up at him. "Brady," she whispered.

"Marry me, Susanna?" he asked.

She leaned into his big, warm body. "Let's do it soon."

He kissed her then. "Things will change around here. I'll build you a bigger and better house, and I think we could remodel the garage you've been living in. Add a second story, more windows, maybe a deck. It would be a good artist's studio for when you want to paint or just dream."

For a few seconds, staring into his eyes, listening to the love in his voice, Susanna couldn't speak. Finally she found the words she needed to say. "You are the most wonderful of men, and... I love the fact that you would do this for me, but you don't have to. I don't care about the buildings as long as I have you."

"You have me, and you have my heart."

And he kissed her. When they finally broke apart, they were both smiling. "Everyone in town is going to be so happy," she told him. "We should go tell them. I think some of them are still here."

He nodded. "Where's our baby?"

Susanna blinked. She closed her eyes to hold in the joy for a second, them opened them to behold the man she loved, the miracle she had found waiting for her in Red Rose. "The baby we already have is with Lydia. Our other babies are still in my dreams."

She could see Brady visibly swallowing. She knew that her words had made him happy. But suddenly he slipped his thumb beneath her chin and stared into her eyes. "I want you to know…our children don't have to take the name Malone. You don't have to take it, either."

Susanna pushed herself to her feet. She wanted to be standing when she said this. She didn't want to be touching him, because she wanted him to know that her head was clear. "I'm already a Malone in my heart, Brady, and of course my children will bear your name. This town hasn't seen the last of the Malones. The line is going to multiply. I'm sure of it. I'm…I'm feeling very fertile," she added, looking for some oomph to end her impassioned speech.

Brady rose to meet her. He tipped back his head and laughed. He took her into his arms. "Susanna, I have a definite feeling that the luck of the Malones has just changed. And you know something else?"

"What?"

"Lon is right. I once had a dream and I lost it, but this new dream of a life with you and our children is so much better than anything I ever imagined."

"It's much better than anything I ever imagined, too," she confessed, "and I have a very active imagination. Come on, Brady." She tugged on his hand.

"Where are we going?" he asked.

"We're going to get Grace and then we're going to tell everyone in town our good news. The Malones are here in Red Rose to stay, and they're very much in love." Susanna pulled on the door, and several women nearly fell in.

She looked back at Brady and he laughed. "Welcome ladies," he said. "And gentlemen." He nodded to Lon and the other men that were there.

"So?" Delia asked, glaring at Susanna.

Susanna frowned, confused. "So?" she asked.

"So is he staying?" Sunny asked. "For Pete's sake, tell us already. The tension is killing me."

Brady nodded to the crowd.

"He's staying," Brady said, "and so is his bride-to-be." Then he took Susanna in his arms and kissed her in front of all of his new friends in Red Rose.

* * * * *

In a Fairy Tale World...
Six reluctant couples. Five classic love stories.
One matchmaking princess.
And time is running out!

Don't miss
THEIR LITTLE COWGIRL by Myrna Mackenzie,
the first tale in this magical miniseries.
Coming in October 2004
only from Silhouette Books.

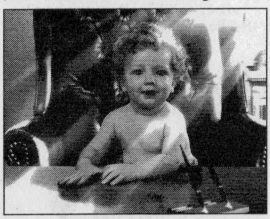

If you enjoyed what you just read,
then we've got an offer you can't resist!

Take 2 bestselling love stories FREE!

Plus get a FREE surprise gift!

SILHOUETTE Romance

COMING NEXT MONTH

#1726 HER SECOND-CHANCE MAN—Cara Colter

High school outsider Jessica Moran could never forget golden boy Brian Kemp's teasing smile—or the unlikely friendship they'd shared when she'd helped him heal a sick dog. So when Brian walked back into her life fourteen years later, with another sick puppy and a rebellious teenager in tow, Jessica knew she was being given a second chance at love....

#1727 CINDERELLA'S SWEET-TALKING MARINE—Cathie Linz

Men of Honor

Captain Ben Kozlowski was a marine with a mission! Sworn to protect the sister of a fallen soldier, he marched into Ellie Jensen's life and started issuing orders. But this sassy single mother had some rules of her own, and before long, Ben found himself wanting to promise to love and honor more than to serve and protect.

#1728 CALLIE'S COWBOY—Madeline Baker

When Native American rancher Cade Kills Thunder came to her rescue on a remote Montana highway, Callie Walker was in heaven. The man was even more handsome than the male models that graced the covers of her romance novels! Would Callie be able to capture this rugged rancher's attention...and his heart?

#1729 THE BOSS'S BABY SURPRISE—Lilian Darcy

Soulmates

Cecilia Rankin kept having the weirdest dreams, like visions of her sexy boss, Nick Delaney, soothing a crying child. But when her dream began to come true and Nick ended up guardian of his sister's baby, Celie knew that Nick really *was* the man of her dreams.